Chicken Coop
for a Rubber Sole

Humours short stories of everyday life

COL. LAYTON PARK

EDITED BY

ARLENE PRUNKL AND JESSI HOFFMAN

iUniverse, Inc.
Bloomington

Chicken Coop for a Rubber Sole
Humours short stories of everyday life

iUniverse books may be ordered through booksellers or by contacting:

iUniverse
1663 Liberty Drive
Bloomington, IN 47403
www.iuniverse.com
1-800-Authors (1-800-288-4677)

ISBN: 978-1-4502-4114-4 (sc)
ISBN: 978-1-4502-4115-1 (ebk)

Printed in the United States of America

iUniverse rev. date: 05/27/2011

Chicken Coop
for a Rubber Sole

CONTENTS

Introduction

I love to tell stories, and, like Aesop, I believe there is a lesson in most of them. For years I shared my stories with my friends and family, who told me I have a warped outlook on life. They gave me numerous suggestions about what I should do with my stories, and although a few responses were anatomically impossible, the stories contained in this book have received positive feedback. I hope you enjoy reading them as much as the readers who chose them for this collection.

One person suggested the collection would make a great bathroom book. Being from a ranch in the foothills of Alberta, I know people who still have bathroom books. One friend told me, however, that since Sears began printing catalogues on slick glossy paper, they have not been as useful as the old newsprint versions were as bathroom books. Knowing this, I was a little insulted at first imagining folks pulling pages from my book in which to wrap their outhouse experiences. The person explained that was not what she'd had in mind. She said her husband would enjoy my stories for their humour. Also, they were shorter than those in *Reader's Digest* so it might free up more bathroom time for the rest of the family.

In the beginning, I didn't have a clue about how to get a book published or how to market these stories. My wife, Myrna, suggested I start by contacting newspaper editors, and TJ at the small monthly publication for almost seniors, *North of Fifty* was the first to print some of them. Soon I had an ongoing humour column in that periodical. Later, *Western Native News*, *Alberta Native News*, *The Okanagan Business Journal*, *The RCMP Quarterly*, *Rocky Mountaineer*, and others also ran some.

I began to think a column musing on everyday mishaps and adventures as seen through my twisted vision might be fun. After all, I already have one fan ("Hi Mom") and hoped others would enjoy the stories as well. The topics would range from my experiences in business, speaking, traveling, and early "retirement," thoughts on the news of the day, the trials of a stay-at-home Dad, and any other topic that I thought readers might find entertaining.

People wondered how I would keep the flow of stories coming. What if my imagination ran dry? But new, fresh material was always at hand. My eldest daughter, Katherine, had just graduated from university and was entering the work force, and her younger sister, Shauna, had given me my first granddaughter, Kierra, and grandson, Easton. Our two boys, Carson and Liam, were in high school, as was our niece, Janine, who also lived with us. Every day there was a new crisis in our household. Come to think of it, perhaps the advantages of Planned Parenthood would make a good story, although I'm not sure whether I'm qualified to be the one to write about it.

At a recent talk, I mentioned that I used to speak on my five theories on how to raise perfect children, but now I have five children and no theories. At the end of the talk, a psychologist approached me and asked if I could send her a copy of my theories. It just shows you how anyone can play psychologist. People say that my sometimes-twisted sense of humor goes over people's heads. If that is your case, may I suggest that you read the book while standing, but not while in the bathroom. But I digress . . .

In the event that I should run out of adventures, trivia, and other useless information, I hope you, the readers, will also help by sending me your stories and suggestions. In any event, as Ted Kennedy once said, "We'll cross that bridge when we come to it."

This was my first book of humourous short stories, compiled from my newspaper columns. If you like it, tell your friends . . . and if you don't, please send it to a poor rancher for his outhouse.

Enjoy!

Col. Layton Park

Layton met the governor of Kentucky who presented him with the honorary title of Colonel. Still he complains that the wife won't curtsy to him and the boys weren't impressed when they discovered they still had to pay full price for fried chicken. It is an honor however that Layton is very proud to have been awarded.

1 · Why Chicken Coop?

This book was published under the title *Chicken Coop for a Rubber Sole* as it was a collection of short funny or inspirational stories and is sort of a parody to the *Chicken Soup for the Soul* books.

Needing clarification, I looked up *parody*. According to Merriam-Webster's Online Dictionary, it means "a literary work in which the style of an author or work is closely imitated for comic effect or in ridicule."

Comic effect? I worried if Jack Canfield or Mark Victor Hansen discovered the book, would they see the humour in it or would their lawyers advise them otherwise? As the book became popular I decided that it should be renamed *Park on the Edge*, one of a collection of works that play on my own name, however my editor thought otherwise so here it is, the second edition of Chicken Coop.

The reason I originally created the parody began in 1987, when my wife Myrna and I flew our airplane to Red Deer to attend a real estate sales rally.

A delayed flight meant the speaker would arrive in Calgary at 10:00 a.m., an hour after he was to be on stage. The head of the rally knew I had an aircraft and asked if I would mind flying to Calgary and return him to Red Deer in order to save time. Myrna and I were interested in speaking and training as a career, so we were happy to do that in order to talk personally with the speaker.

On the return flight, he shared his belief system, which included the theory that we should all live at the level we desire, and the money will follow. He went on to explain that he had gone through a financial crisis with little remaining but his most expensive asset: a thousand-dollar suit and monogrammed shirt. He said it is important to look and feel the part of being successful.

He said in his mind he was a millionaire . . . it was just that the money had not shown up yet. I found it strange that he was making a living speaking about success to business people . . . most of whom were likely better off financially than he was.

After his presentation, he convinced us to buy his new self-published book, called "My Future Diary," which was a guide on how to write your goals as though they had already been achieved. "Interesting," I thought to myself, and handed it to Myrna, who completed the mini-workbook on our flight home.

We had an opportunity to meet with the same speaker a number of times over the next few years. The last time was in the early 1990's, when a local business person arranged for him to visit our city. Later, we all went out for supper, and Myrna brought her copy of the book, which she confessed she had not looked at since that flight home years before.

To her our amazement, we had achieved almost every goal she had written in it. What really surprised us was a picture she had drawn of how she envisioned her dream house. Although I had not seen the drawing, I had just finished designing and building a house for us that looked surprisingly like the picture she had drawn, complete with triangular windows.

The speaker was very interested in the story and offered us copies of his newest book. He told us his goal was to have it become a bestseller and that he already had titles to forty sequels. He even shared some of the titles, which I thought to be somewhat corny. I recall my scepticism as I thought he would be lucky if he ever had one best-seller, but fortunately, I kept my thoughts to myself and instead admired the confidence he had in his vision.

A couple of months later I was sitting in our real estate office when I overheard a woman talking to the receptionist at the front desk. She introduced herself as the new manager of a local radio station, and I was intrigued when she insisted, "I have to meet Myrna."

When the receptionist showed the woman into our common office, she began shaking Myrna's hand vigorously, saying, "I'm so excited to meet you. I just have to know how you've become so well connected."

The woman then related how she had attended a course in New York City, and the speaker had floored her when he talked about goal setting. He said his friend Myrna Park from Grande Prairie, Alberta, had successfully used his techniques. He then relayed the story about the house.

The woman finished by saying she could not believe she'd travelled all the way to the Big Apple to hear a speaker talk about someone who worked just blocks away from her station.

"Not only that," she added, "His latest book, *Chicken Soup for the Soul*, is well on its way to becoming a best-seller."

Mark Victor Hansen's books have now achieved unparalleled success, and he and Jack Canfield must have published the forty titles or more Mark had initially envisioned.

Mark has kindly endorsed the corporate and personal training programs Myrna and I offer and gave us quotes for the back covers of other books we have published. I wrote to him prior to naming this book and asked for a comment about my new book, Get Out of Your Way, but the gatekeeper at Mark's office informed me that Mark no longer endorsed books.

We had provided our aviation fuel, Myrna's story for him to use, and our entertaining company, I thought a quick note was reasonable. (Is keeping score for twenty years a little obsessive on my part? Yes, but it is my book, so I can write what I want.)

I would have been flattered to receive a comment even if his note said only that the book was softer than the Sears catalogue and a wise addition to any outhouse.

So, tongue-in-cheek, I came up with the title *Chicken Coop for a Rubber Sole*, for this book thinking imitation is the best form of flattery. I greatly admire what Jack and Mark have accomplished, but Mark once told me it is easier to ask for forgiveness than permission, so Mark please forgive me.

Then as the book went to print the first time, Mark had the last laugh as he sent me an endorsment for *Get Out of Your Way*. Knowing Marks sense of humour I decided to keep the title anyway.

I hope you enjoy reading it as much as I did living it.

Layton and Myrna with Mark Victor Hansen
(Author of Chicken Soup for the Soul series)
Showing their matching cowboy boots in 2007

2 · Stay Young Forever

"What advice do you have for those who haven't yet become fifty or are in transition? And yes, how about some tips and tricks on how to stay young forever, that would be cool."

~ Email from Greta in response to my humour column in *North of Fifty*.

Well, Greta, my immediate response is another question: why are you reading this magazine? It is restricted; you have to be over fifty. That is one of the rules, but then I've heard there are lots of you youngsters out there picking it up on the sly and peeking inside it in the privacy of your bedrooms. That's why they decided to drop the centrefold feature (wouldn't you know, just a month short of my turn). Now it will be like *Playboy* and people will only buy it for the articles. And it's no use bombarding the editor with letters of requests asking for my spread, either. She says she has made up her mind. I think she cancelled it because at six-foot-three, I did not fit on the centre spread and it was going to require an expensive extra foldout section. Now it will be like *Playboy* and people will only buy it for the articles.

However, as long as you are reading the paper, I may as well impart to you the secrets of staying young.

The first thing, Greta, is you that you must eliminate the word *cool* from your vocabulary. Heck, that makes you sound my age, especially if you have the urge to follow it with *rad* or *fab*. Instead, insert the word *like*, about every five to ten words, like, you know what I mean?

You will also want to find a way to make a younger statement without saying anything. Tattoos are, like, where it's at now. It's best to get one that shows just above some private part you don't want people looking at. When folks strain to see whether it is a tattoo or something crawling from where it shouldn't be, you can raise your voice and say, "Hey, what the * * * (this magazine isn't young enough to use the right words here) are you looking at anyway?" Of course, getting it placed in precisely the right spot is tricky because current fashion trends dictate there be less and less room between the private parts of the body and where the clothes end.

Choosing the right tattoo is important. If it is too big and you can see too much, it takes away from the mystery and people will not be interested in looking.

On the other hand, if you move it closer to a private part, well, like, I ain't letting some three-hundred-pound biker and part time tattoo artist with a power needle get that close to any of my privates, if you know what I mean.

You may want to consider the pierced look instead, and I don't mean something as old-fashioned as a dozen earrings in each ear.

Eyebrow rings are good. They say, "Hey, look at me. I'm soooo bad."

The nose is passé unless you have a chain going from it to one ear. Add a tongue stud and your unspoken message screams, "Hey . . . I look more unemployable than you do." If you cannot afford the tongue stud right away, put two small rocks in your mouth so when you talk, folks will think you have one.

Guys, you could have the old ring through the centre of the nose to look bullish. But it doesn't make you look young so you may only attract old cows, I mean the ones with the tags still in their ears, bells around their necks, and a cigarette between their hooves.

I would get a piercing myself if it didn't hurt. I don't even like visiting the dentist, so how could I live through having a bellybutton ring installed? Besides, unless I get one the size of a Buick hubcap, you wouldn't be able to see it.

According to what I read, they have now pierced almost every part of the body. I like to be on the cutting edge, so the only places left that I can think of that will not hurt are my big toes, where I won't know the difference between the pain and gout, or through the calluses on my heels, but then who will ever see them?

I find it easier to hang around with guys who are ten to fifteen years older than me and a woman ten years younger with a large, permanent smile. Compared with the guys, I look younger, and when folks see me with a younger woman wearing a big smile, well, it leaves them thinking. While we're on the subject, I would like to give the waitresses over at IHOP a tip. I eat there Monday mornings with Mike and Dave, who, incidentally, are not the same old guys I was talking about.

Anyway, the waitresses are usually quite good to us, but recently I had a birthday and noticed that according to the menu I now qualify for the seniors' discount meal. So I ordered it. The waitress took my order and never batted an eye. There was no "May I see some ID, please?" Do you know how humiliating that is for someone who thinks they are still twenty-something?

Would it have been too much for her to say, "My, you don't look like a senior citizen!" So I did what any good senior would do: I left her a twenty-three-cent tip.

3. The East Coast Ghost

Do you believe in ghosts? I didn't used to, but the following story is absolutely true and l wanted to share the experience with you.

The wife and I had a chance to visit the East Coast on a business trip at Halloween. We added an extra week to our visit so we could explore Nova Scotia, staying at various bed and breakfasts. Being a prairie boy, I was intrigued by lighthouses, so the wife found a B&B that had one on the property. We arrived late in the day and explored the 150-year-old building. Still later, we spent the evening with the owners, Mr. and Mrs. Kent, who related the following story to us.

Mr. Kent's great-grandfather had built the home on the property in the early 1800s. He had served eighteen years as first officer and sailed Lord Nelson's ship back to England after Nelson's death at the battle of Trafalgar. The British government rewarded great-grandfather Kent for his service by giving him command of his own ship, then sent him to Canada to fight in the War of 1812. He became a war hero raiding American ships. After a sword injury to his leg forced him to resign his commission in the British Navy, he retired and purchased the property where we were now staying.

Captain Kent built a small house next to the lighthouse. Local folklore claimed that the house became occupied by an unknown presence. Twenty years later, the captain destroyed the house and built the new one where we were lodged for the night. According to the legend, the spirit moved from the old house to the lighthouse, where numerous sightings were reported.

A few years ago, during another Halloween, a vehicle caused a stir when all its lights began to flash and the horn began honking steadily and would not quit. A report on the incident made the news and a clairvoyant arrived from New York to investigate. After spending some time in the lighthouse alone, she told Mr. Kent she had experienced a "presence." Without knowing the history, she said she did not understand why he was at this particular place, but the ghost was that

8

of Lord Admiral Nelson. The Kents believe his spirit had come to the new land with his protégé, Captain Kent, and remains there to this day.

We knew the East Coast was rife with such stories and found it amusing, but of course, we never really believed it. It was soon time for bed, and I headed to the room. The wife went out to retrieve her overnight bag which she had left in the rental car.

The ocean was calm. The only light came from a beam from the lighthouse, throwing its cautionary message into the blackness to warn passing ships. The beam from the lighthouse added to the eerie mood created by the chill, the silence, and the darkness. The setting could not have been more appropriate for what was about to happen.

After getting her bag, she closed the trunk and started back for the house when she heard a click and turned to see the lid pop open. She was sure it had latched. Still, she shrugged and returned to slam the lid down again.

As she walked away a second time, she heard the trunk spring open again and a wave of goose bumps ran up her arms and down her back. She looked back at the car but saw nothing. She strained to look out into the dark, but all was still.

Slowly, she walked back and lifted the lid. The trunk was empty. There was no reason for the lid not to shut tight and latch. She slammed it down hard a third time and made sure that it firmly latched before starting back to the house.

Before she had taken two steps, she heard the lid pop again. Nervously, she turned around and quickly shut it hard and leaned against it, holding it down for what seemed like more than a few long seconds. Nothing happened. It was definitely closed this time.

As she stood alone looking around, something moved and caught her attention. She looked up at a second storey-window of the old house. There was something or someone there, behind the dark and dirty glass, and it was staring at her. She could feel it. Straining to see through the window, she could identify an outline. Then something happened that she would never forget.

Through the dark glass of the old house, she began to make out a bearded figure. As she watched, it began to raise its right arm. She was paralyzed with fear. She watched as the arm continued to rise. It seemed to be pointing at her! A cold wave of air came from nowhere, flooding over her, freezing her to the spot. The arm was now fully extended toward her.

Just then, the beam from the lighthouse raced across the side of the house and hit the window, lighting up my face. I had been exposed! I stood there, a grin spreading over my face as I held the remote control unit that opened the trunk.

We are not sure where our next adventure will be, but I'm sure, wherever it is, that I will be responsible for retrieving all the luggage from the car!.

4 · Home Invasion

When we moved to the Okanagan (a Native word meaning *a great place to retire*), one of the things I most looked forward to was welcoming company from back home. My new neighbour, Fred, could not understand my enthusiasm for visitors. He warned me that anyone I had ever nodded hello to back on the prairies would turn up at our home looking for a free Okanagan holiday if I didn't nip it in the bud.

"Don't encourage them," Fred cautioned, "or you'll be running a hotel." He said that people from Saskatchewan (another Native word, which means *you cannot jump to your death here*) make especially bad visitors. "If the flatlanders make it through the twisting mountain roads, they are often too frightened to return, so they stay, some forever."

I laughed, but Fred was serious. "Do the math," he said. "There are more retired people from Weyburn, Rosetown, and Moose Jaw living in the Okanagan than the entire population of all three places put together."

Wanting to be helpful, Fred offered a few suggestions to curb the flow of prairie traffic to our home. "We keep two suitcases in the closet beside the front door," he said. "When someone shows up and there is any indication they may be planning to stay, we pretend we are just getting ready to go out of town for a few days. You'd better have a good plan, too."

Apparently, Fred felt his message wasn't sinking in, so he testified. "One time, some people showed up whom I hardly knew, so I pulled the suitcase trick. Instead of leaving, they asked if they could use the house anyway. We ended up staying at a motel for the weekend. Now we keep clothes in the suitcases."

The topic of out-of-town visitors continued to pop up, and I learned of several new tricks one of which is leaving only one roll of toilet paper in the guest bathroom. The idea is that after you continually promise to replenish the empty roll (but never do), the unwanted guests will find accommodation somewhere else, rather than embarrass you by reminding you yet again. Or they may just buy their own toilet paper.

Another helpful neighbour suggested we register our home as a bed and breakfast and post a sign on the back door: Rooms for rent—$150 per night. Sometimes that alone will make uninvited guests feel guilty, and they will depart. If that doesn't work, you still have the option of saying, "We'd love to have you stay, but unfortunately, all of the rooms are booked after Wednesday."

I suspect our neighbours thought we were crazy. I was so pleased at the idea of getting company that I visited a local furniture store to buy a fold-out couch for extra sleeping quarters. The salesperson asked if I wanted the one-night bed, the weekender, or the full-week bed. The confused look on my face prompted an explanation.

"Sofa beds are available in three different models," the salesman explained, "the one-nighter is a bed fitted with a bar that runs across the lumbar position, making for a very uncomfortable sleep. Stiffness is guaranteed after only one night, prompting guests to leave the following day." He smiled and continued.

"The weekender has the same bar but a thicker mattress and additional padding so aches and stiffness don't show up for two or three nights. It is only moderately uncomfortable, designed for those you want to visit but not to overstay their welcome." He paused for effect.

"The full-week bed is for close family or friends whom you want to come for a short stay, but not move in. It features the same construction but the bar drops in the middle of the bed and it has even more padding. It has no negative effect but is uncomfortable enough to keep guests from enjoying a really good night's sleep. After several nights, they, too, will decide to move on."

"The beds may not have been designed with those particular purposes in mind," the salesperson explained, "but here in the valley, that's how we rate them. It's the only way to keep control over your home."

After some discussion, Myrna and I decided against buying a sofabed. She has more out-of-town relatives than I do, so we purchased a foldout futon instead.

We still welcome our prairie friends, but should you ever find us at the front door with our suitcases in hand, you will know we have finally reached our quota of vacationing visitors.

5 · The Sex Diet

The best-selling books are diet books and cookbooks. They do well because they really promote sex, and sex is what sells everything.

Cookbooks tell you how to make meals romantic enough to impress members of the opposite sex (as if she will want to jump into your sack at the mere taste of your flambé); diet books tell you if you were thinner you would look younger and sexier.

Of course, diet cookbooks win on both counts. The clear message is that if we do a good job with either, or both, we will get more sex. In fact, we will buy just about anything if we think it will result in a) more sex, or b) looking sexier. As a result, the public is ready—no, anxious—to learn about the sex diet.

I have studied a number of diets and I am amazed at how many contradict one another. There are high-fat and low-carbohydrate diets. There are high-carbohydrate and low-fat diets. There are diets that allow both as long as they are not consumed at the same time. Diets that dictate what you can eat based on your blood type. Diets that suggest you can eat as much as you want and anything you want as long as you have a glass of water between each bite. And so on. They all claim to work, and they are all popular. Each week the grocery store checkout stand displays numerous books and magazines touting the latest, greatest diet, right there where you can pick up a copy conveniently along with your Laura Secord cake, case of cola, and a gargantuan chocolate bar.

The old model of yesterday's grey-haired, out-of-shape fifty-year-old is long gone, and we boomers are obsessed with searching for the magic that will make us look eternally youthful. We want to be as sexy as some of our fifty—or sixty-something movie heroes, like Cher, Glenn Close, or Dustin Hoffman. Why is it that plastic surgery seems to allow women to stay young and beautiful forever while men turn out looking like Michael Jackson?

Based on the number of gurus showing us the way, I have come to the conclusion that anyone can call themselves an expert on the most effective way to lose weight by simply inventing their own program, so here is mine. I call it the Sex Diet.

It's called the Sex Diet for two reasons. First, because sex is really the outcome we are in search of, so the name has real marketing potential. Second, on my diet you can eat anything you want, as long as you eat it only while having sex. Don't laugh. After all, who craves potato chips while playing slap and tickle? Most cravings disappear as soon as you remove your clothing. In fact, for some it is too much bother to undress for a snack, so unless you enjoy sex with your clothes on, the amount eaten will be immediately reduced.

Those who are willing to strip down find that suddenly the thought of eating disappears or the types of food they desire suddenly changes. Gone are the cravings for over processed, high-calorie foods. One look in the mirror and your brain is probably screaming, "Diet food!" Immediately, and without any conscious thought, cravings shift to more natural food items. The next time you are being intimate, ask yourself: Would I sooner have a big plate of spaghetti right now or a banana? Even if you unwittingly choose the spaghetti, are you going to "take a break" to make it? Besides, you simply can't eat that much pasta while frolicking through the covers.

There is a lot to be said for this diet. While the thought of whipping cream may still be exciting to some, an electric mixer in bed poses too many dangers for most of us. Ice cream gets ruled out as soon as it touches someplace unfriendly to cold foods. Likewise, buttered popcorn is too messy. Anything that requires a knife, fork or other sharp utensil tends to cause a loss of concentration. Popsicles not only fit into the cold category, but if the sticks are flung about carelessly in the heat of the moment, you could lose an eye. (Let that happen just once, and you can imagine the warning labels government will demand be printed on the wrappers.)

Foods that suit this program are limited to those that can be eaten with one hand, do not require utensils, and are not crumbly or sticky. Hot foods can cause as much anxiety as cold foods. Delivered foods are an option, but you know that pizza is going to show up at exactly the wrong time. There is no denying the effectiveness of this diet. You are probably already looking forward to your next meal.

For those who can't wait to buy a copy of my *Sex Diet* book, I make this humble offer. If enough of you send me $19.95 for a copy, I will actually sit down and write it.

6 · The Tasting

Myrna is very involved as a community volunteer. Recently she, along with her friend Carol Lee, began to organize the President's Ball. The event was the prestigious annual fundraiser for a local college, and the women attacked the project with great vigour. This was the formal event of the year, and they left nothing to chance, choosing and hanging the dramatic black-and-white decorations themselves. Maintaining the same colour theme, tables were adorned with black tablecloths and white centrepieces. Even the band and catering staff would be dressed in black tuxedoes, white shirts, and black bow ties.

The final task was to choose the wine, and the women invited their husbands to assist. I reluctantly agreed. Carol Lee's husband, Jack, an English gentleman who fancied himself an expert on all cultural subjects, instantly accepted.

The women also asked Turk to be a committee member. Turk's thick hands and weathered features divulged the years he had spent working his way through the ranks from a field hand to head of the area's largest resource company. As the largest employer in the community, his name was on the invitation list for most fundraising events. and he was proud to attend.

Darrel, owner of a local wine store, offered to host the tasting for the committee. The six gathered for the selection process.

"I'm happy to see you here," I said as Darrel joined Turk in the wine-tasting room. "I don't know much about wine-tasting, and I'm a little nervous."

"I can only tell the difference between red and white wine if I can see them," Turk replied. "I came only because I heard they were going to serve my two favourite wines, red and free."

While Darrel was a wine connoisseur by way of his business, Jack had become a self-proclaimed expert through years of self-delusion.

Darrel had prepared a spreadsheet listing several wines down the left column and headings across the top including bouquet, taste, colour, clarity, flavour, sweetness, body, and so on for each committee member. Darrel carefully poured the first wine. Then he and Jack, accepting the serious responsibility of the task before them, hoisted their glasses up to the light and swirled them expertly, before jotting notes on their sheets. A thoroughly confused Turk looked in his glass, then at me, and shrugged.

The two "experts" plunged their noses into the glasses, inhaling deeply and throwing their heads back almost in unison. They stood with eyes closed, faces pointed skyward, savouring the bouquet. They scribbled more notes as the four of us looked on.

Then, again in unison, Jack and Darrel each took a sip, swished the wine around in their mouths and spit it out, smacking their lips. They rinsed their palettes with clean, cold water and added more notes.

The two women looked at each other, sipped, held the wine in their mouths, maximizing the full taste sensation, and then they swallowed.

Turk looked at me, shot back the entire glass, wiped his lips with the back of his hand and nodded in approval as a refreshing "ahhh" slipped out. I promptly followed suit.

Darrel charged glasses from a new bottle, and the process started over with a verbal competition that quickly escalated between the experts, Jack and Darrel.

Darrel stated the next wine had a full bouquet but the flavour was round, almost too "vegetabley."

Jack opined that the wine had fine clarity and continued with a vivid and detailed description. The women remained silent.

"That one had good bite!" Turk interjected, but Jack and Darrel took no notice and continued to compete for centre court.

"This is a little sharp, don't you think?"

"This vintage seems a little overpowering."

"That one had good legs."

"This one has a spicy nose."

And several were too fruity.

As the competition for the right description increased, the comments became more absurd.

"The grapes in this wine were picked after the first frost."

"These grapes came from the south side of the hill."

Turk attempted to get in on the debate. "I think that one has higher alcohol content." He belched and refilled his glass, offering me one, which I readily accepted.

Finally, after sampling all the wines, Darrel asked authoritatively, "Has everyone completed scoring their sheets?"

"Perhaps Carol Lee and Myrna should state their choices first," Jack suggested. "After all, it is their event."

The other men signaled their agreement. A moment of silence followed as Myrna considered her options.

"Well…" she started hesitantly, "I think the wine in the black bottles with the white labels would look the best on the black tablecloths. What do you think, Carol Lee?"

"I absolutely agree," Carol replied. Being an interior designer, she would know best when it comes to that kind of thing.

Jack and Darrel were speechless until Turk offered a sensible suggestion.

"Maybe we should taste them all one more time, just to be sure."

Meet the Family—Part 1

It seemed a shame to waste the extra pages where a story doesn't finish at the bottom of the page, so I thought I would use this space throughout to introduce you to members of my family and share some of their funny stories.

In the fall of 1996 while I was away, Myrna was invited, as president of the Real Estate Board, to attend a supper with the premier of Alberta, Ralph Klein.

The boys (six and four) weren't used to Mom going out alone when Dad was away, and they began questioning where she was going to.

Myrna found it difficult to explain who the premier was, so she asked if they knew who the kings were in their storybooks. They said they did.

"The Premier is sort of like the king of Alberta," she explained, "and I'm going to a supper with a lot of other people to welcome him to our town." The boys were impressed and satisfied, so they granted their approval.

Later that night Myrna had an opportunity to tell the story to "Ralph," who thought it amusing. In a demonstration of how laid-back he really was, he took the time to write a note to the boys on the back of the program and signed, "from King Ralph . . . (Klein) . . . Premier."

I am of the opinion that any kids who are on a first-name basis with a King should be listened to. Perhaps they have lessons for all of us. Thus I began recording some of their more philosophical comments and stories to share with you.

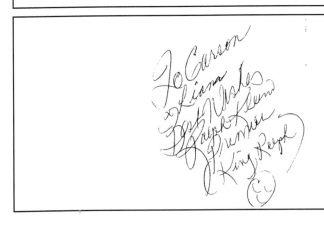

7 · Who Designed the Stores?

After years of shopping for groceries, I still find it a struggle. I can spend two hours looking for a left-handed, fine-thread, hardened, galvanized number-eight screw, but there is nothing exciting to look at in a food store. I mean, one can of peas pretty much looks the same as another can, and you either want one or you don't.

In the past, when I had to buy groceries, I would just grab the most familiar brands: Campbell's soups, Heinz ketchup, French's mustard, and Kraft cheese. Why spend time worrying or scheming on how to save twelve cents by purchasing some unknown label? After all, TV tells us the best value is in those familiar brands.

That approach was okay when I was trusted to go out for a few items, but when I became the primary shopper spending hundreds of dollars; I had to learn the rules. After all, saving just 10 percent on $200 is another $20.

One of the first challenges was learning how to find things. Grocery stores are not laid out as a man thinketh, yet Myrna told me it was men who originally designed them. Designed, it seems, so customers would have to walk past the slow–moving, healthier items in order to reach the faster–moving, but not-so-healthy ones.

That explains why the milk is always at the back of the store. No wonder the system doesn't make sense! Only a marketing person would come up with that plan. Women, of course, understand those sneaky marketers and rather than change them, they have evolved and adapted to them.

Men, however, are logical, and as most women know, do not adapt quickly. If a normal, logical guy were to design the store layout, the wieners, buns, ketchup, and mustard would all be on the same shelf. In fact, we would allow grocery stores to sell beer and we would put it in this same row next to the barbeque sauce. The milk and sugar would be in the cereal aisle and bread and butter would be with the butter and the jam.

We would have the aisles go only one way, like some streets, and be wide enough for two of the oversized buggies to pass safely. The two-way aisles always cause traffic jams as people stop and talk to an approaching friend, study a can of peas, or they simply wander around in a fog thinking about how exciting it might be to put anchovies in the salad for a change.

Having everyone travelling in the same direction would make it easier to remain friendly to other shoppers.

"Good afternoon," I say politely on the first aisle when I meet another shopper. I think the world is too cold and I enjoy extending a good word whenever I can. Then at the end of the aisle, I turn the corner and start down the next one.

"Hi, again," I say with a smile as I pass the same shopper again on aisle two. By aisle ten, we do not look at each other anymore. Me, because I've just run out of greetings, friendly or otherwise; they, because they think I'm nuts to be talking to a stranger in the first place.

I thought I would never get the hang of grocery shopping. I would often wander the aisles in a daze, lulled by the elevator music. Actually, I resent these songs being called elevator music, as many of them were cutting-edge, wild rock when they were first recorded in the sixties. Now they play these great tunes in commercials to link them to various products, so when we hear them in the store we are encouraged to buy the product.

It is disillusioning to hear your childhood heroes pushing commercial products. Thank God for some of the old holdouts like the Stones. You do not hear Rogers' commercials playing to the sound of Brown Sugar in the background, although if a face cream manufacturer could take a hundred years off of Keith Richards' face, it would be a winner, and Mick's dancing could be used for either Viagra or Depends. But again I digress.

I continue struggling to find the items I need. Hundreds of bright packages distract me as they compete for my attention, but I swear that even if it takes me hours to find all the items on my list, I will uphold the code of real men and not ask for directions.

As more of us real men take up the responsibility of shopping, we will rise up together and revolt. We will demand that the retailers listen to us and begin putting things in a logical order where they belong, like the hemorrhoid cream next to the toilet paper.

8 · Life in the Fast Lane

When I was young, I wanted it all; I was quick and ambitious and was certain that one day I would be in the fast lane.

I never quite made it, although I did retire early and spent a couple of years as a stay-at-home dad, which presented several new challenges. I mastered many things such as learning to turn on a vacuum cleaner and learning to can the fruit from our trees, but the one task I never mastered was the art of shopping. Like so many of life's lessons, I learned what I know in the alley, albeit the alley between the canned corn and the pickles.

When I say shopping, I do not mean wandering through a store looking for deals. I can cruise a hardware store for hours sniffing out bargains on nail straighteners and other good things I might need someday. I am talking about shopping for food.

I never saw why going to the grocery store should be a big deal. In fact, I could never understand how my wife could take so long to buy a few morsels to eat. It is not like wandering through Canadian Tire, where there are hundreds of fun gadgets and interesting products to inspect.

Women outperform men in this field; I'm convinced it must be genetic. I mean, men just don't pick it up naturally the way women do. For example, last week I saw a fellow approaching with a half-full cart, and as we met, I recognized that he was indeed a high roller, someone of importance, a man on the run. You know the type I mean. He was dressed in an Armani suit, well-groomed, and he had all the right accessories.

He hardly slowed as he plucked items from the shelves with his left hand while continuing to talk into a miniature cell phone in his right which sported more rings and bracelets than a small jewellery store. I wondered if he was buying or selling stock, checking on investment property with his realtor, arranging airline tickets, or simply talking to his tailor.

In the next aisle we both stopped in front of the cheese, and suddenly I became aware of his conversation. It seemed an unseen controller was guiding him through the store. I tried to look thoughtful, as if I might have forgotten something; then I turned around and followed him.

Like a pilot on a tricky instrument approach, he received his instructions through his communication device and reacted accordingly. It was truly a beautiful sight—precision flying that only ground control and a pilot together could produce. He glided from section to section picking out the correct items, and then moved on. I tried to keep up, but I could not find my items fast enough.

While he soared through the store, I fumbled with the list, looking for the items that might be located in this row, then realizing I had missed two items from the previous row. I was jealous as I raced to keep up. Finally, it occurred to me that the only way he could be reaching this speed was if there was a woman as the controller on the other end of the phone. Somewhere she sat, seeing the supermarket in her mind like some sort of radar screen.

"Maxwell House coffee, two o'clock, top shelf and coming up fast." I could imagine her directions as she guided him down the invisible airways. I was amazed as he flew on, leaving me behind still searching for the premixed pancake flour.

As I lined up at the one open till, I looked out the front window and saw him load the last of his bags in a BMW, right next to my 1972 Fiat. He straightened his tie, got behind the wheel, and sped off, while I looked down at my Wal-Mart shorts and Birkenstock sandals. The closest thing I own to German-engineered transportation.

Ahead of me, forty-three shoppers tapped their fingers in time as they waited for the customer at the till searching his pockets again for his discount card.

I glanced down the long line of empty checkout aisles and saw one shopper unloading a cart at the end, below a sign that said, "Nine Items or Less." I sighed, realizing it would be a long time before I qualified for the fast lane.

9 · The Art of Shopping

I have not always been a journeyman shopper. When I first retired, Myrna continued to work, so she would often send me to the store for a quart of milk and loaf of bread. I would cruise the store to see what else I should buy, partly because we seldom had pickled herring or canned sardines and partly because if I bought a ton of things, I surmised, she would quit sending me.

I would go for a couple of items and return with hundreds of dollars in groceries. The cupboards filled with cases of the same thing because I could not remember if we needed more, but they were on sale so I would buy another case.

Instead of telling me she would do the shopping, Myrna suggested I start using a list. I would stand in the aisle gripping my list with the same feeling I had years ago standing in front of the principal's office with a note from home. In fact, it was worse than that: I felt I must look like a man who had a note allowing me to buy only certain foods. I was sure the checkout clerk would want to see my list then scold me if I tried to buy something that was not on it.

"Put those smoked oysters back!" I could hear the clerk sternly say.

I found myself wandering from one aisle to another scrolling through the list trying to determine if something on it might be hiding in this aisle. I knew I would end up making at least two trips through the store to find all the groceries I missed on the first pass.

As my skills improved, Myrna suggested I should become a journeyman shopper and move to the next level, coupons. It became embarrassing when, at coffee with the guys, instead of pulling out a money clip full of bills, I'd pull out a wad of folded coupons.

I decided to master this task. At first, I would run all over the store picking up only the items in the order I had coupons arranged. That added a couple of kilometres to each trip but time seemed to move faster, or at least I spent less time standing in the middle of the aisle scratching my head and looking lost as I thumbed through the coupons.

It is not easy to organize them, either, as the coupons all come in different sizes. The stores also do not identify themselves on all the coupons, so sometimes I would mix up the coupons from one store with those from another, then spend hours trying to search out the deal the competition was offering.

Out shopping one day, I met my niece Jodi and began proudly showing her my newly acquired skills. I displayed the stack of coupons Myrna had clipped for me. In one hand, I held the coupons for items I had already had, and I flipped through the unused coupons I held in the other.

As I was demonstrating, I noticed one of the little squares did not have anything printed on it. "Strange," I thought, and turned it over to find the coupon was on the other side. Then I turned over the next coupon and found that it, too, had a different item on the other side, as did the next. One by one, I found different coupons on each side of the entire stack. So that explained the baby food and denture paste.

The buggy was full of boxes and cans of things I had never seen in our house before, at least not recently. I had been shopping from the wrong side of the coupons. Frustration set in, and I thought I would never master the skill of shopping. Jodi was less than impressed.

Then, on the day just before Halloween, it happened. I saw piles of candy on sale right inside the entrance, and I remembered we did not have treats for the little goblins. They must really have overstocked to have a pile this high, I thought. I began scooping up bags of bars.

Suddenly, I felt a hand on my elbow and turned to see a woman I did not recognize. She looked around suspiciously to be sure that no one could hear her. At first, I thought she was some sort of covert operator working for the competitor, or perhaps my fly was open, or she had some stolen watches to sell.

Reassured that no one was watching us, she began whispering, "I don't know if you care or not, but these candies are on sale for half price at the grocery store downtown."

"But are they the same brand?" I whispered back, making it sound as if I would never consider giving away no-name brand candies to the kids in my neighbourhood.

"Exactly the same candies as these. These are not on sale, this is a marketing trick," she said under her breath.

I could feel the excitement rising inside as I slowly unloaded my cart, glancing around to ensure those sneaky marketers were not watching. Then I left the store.

Outside, I took a deep breath. "Yes!" I said to myself. "I have arrived." I quietly cheered as I walked to my car realizing the woman had just treated me as an equal. I had become a journeyman shopper.

10 · Home on the Range

My oldest son, Carson, looked up in admiration and said, "This is the best soup in the whole world."

My chest puffed out a little. "Do think your dad is a better cook than the other dads in your school?"

"You make the best soup, Dad," he beamed, hesitating before he added, "but Julian's dad is the best cook."

I'd forgotten about his friend Julian whose father, John, is a first-class chef by profession. I, on the other hand, had just discovered we have a kitchen and had only recently been allowed to use the power appliances. Still, I was proud that I could already prepare three different soups, all of my own creation. Sure I had some help from Campbell's, but I didn't just open cans. I added ingredients and experimented.

Some of my recipes have been so successful I decided it was time I shared my secrets with those of you venturing into the non-professional culinary world.

This was not my first foray into that world; when I was single, there were few cans I couldn't open. But now I was preparing meals for the family, and Myrna had invoked a rule: meals could not be solely from my three favourite food groups, canned, frozen, or take-out. I did not want to let other men down, so I decided to rise to the challenge As they say, this is my story and I am sticking to it. In fact, I pretty much stick to everything in the kitchen.

Men, there are three policies you will want to make note of. First, when you use canned items, hide the evidence at the bottom of the garbage and do not take the garbage out until told to do so or you will raise suspicion.

Second, always add something so you can claim that the can was only one ingredient. I learned this rule following a Christmas dinner I had prepared. I remembered that while growing up, my mother used to make a great raisin glaze for ham. Not wanting to break the basic rule of manhood by using instructions, I ignored all the cookbooks and opened a can of raisin pie filling. It was the talk of the meal, until a snoopy woman tried to squash the garbage down while helping me with the dishes. I was humiliated to see her unearthing the can; then she asked me point blank if this was my wonderful glaze. I managed to convince her it was only *one* of the ingredients.

The third rule is to add brown sugar and garlic to everything. There are no other ingredients that can so magically transform the dullest of foods into succulent dishes. Some of the meals that profit the most include pancakes (skip the garlic here); soups; chilli con carne; stew; or anything with meat, vegetables, or starches in it. If you are short of brown sugar, you cannot go wrong substituting a blob of molasses.

To create the illusion that you have control in the kitchen, learn one or two great dishes for each meal. Eggs Benedict for breakfast are a good example. It's not hard to make, and most women don't have the time to make this brunch favourite, so they are easily impressed, especially if you prime them first with a little champagne and orange juice.

For kids, prepare specially shaped pancakes. They do not have to look that great; the kids' imaginations will take control. For example, when my boys were small, they liked dinosaurs so I made pancakes that looked like dinosaur eggs. Sometimes they could see the reptiles breaking out of them.

Other times they asked for cowboy and Indian pancakes and were thrilled when I created large rocks with the cowboys and Indians hiding behind them. One son could actually see feathers from a headdress peeking over the top of the rocks.

Lunch can be impressive using two unusual soups and a couple of good salads. The soup my boys refer to as "Dad's Famous Soup" is their favourite. Start with a couple of cans of tomato soup diluted with milk. Add a can of Niblet corn, some grated cheese, oregano, and basil. Cut up fried sausage, preferably pepperoni. The soup tastes almost as good as if Julian's dad had made it from scratch. Just remember to hide all the cans carefully, and no one will know the difference.

The secret to a good salad is to add something unusual such as nuts, canned oranges, or pineapple. My rule is: If it does not look or taste familiar, your guests cannot say you made it wrong. Find unusual dressings that you can make in bulk or transplant from their bottle to an old ketchup container you can keep in the fridge.

For supper, learn a special dish and hide the cans that make up the rest of the meal. Always remember that a fancy dessert impresses almost everyone.

Once you have this mastered, guests will consider you a kitchen wizard, but you might find it easier to find new friends than to keep learning new dishes. Just take care to find out who they are first, and make sure John or some other professional chef is not among them.

11 · Traveling in Style

Have you ever yearned to be in the spotlight?

Yearned to have people treat you with respect and gaze at you in wonder? In a small town, arriving in a limousine conjures up that kind of response. Or at least I thought it might.

At one point, I thought it might be fun to drive around in a stretch Cadillac, so when I came across one for sale, I bought it. In order to justify it to Myrna (or should I say, to myself, as Myrna had long ago quit trying to understand some of the things I did), I started a small limousine service.

A special chauffeur's license was required, so whenever I got a call for hire, I called one of the drivers from the funeral home across the street. The rest of the time, I just cruised around in it.

At first, it was a lot of fun. It was the only limo in the city, and people's heads would turn, but after a while I noticed that Myrna and all our friends rode in the back enjoying the trip while I sat up front alone and drove.

One day I got a call from the mayor of Beaverlodge, a small town a few kilometres away. He told me the Lieutenant Governor was flying in to participate in a celebration, and he wanted to hire my limousine to transfer her from the airport to their town and a special anniversary supper. I said I would be pleased to be of service, and we arranged to meet at the airport a half hour early in order for the mayor to brief me on proper protocol.

I know I should have hired a funeral home driver with a proper license, but the Lieutenant Governor had been the province's Solicitor General, or the "top cop" in the province, so I thought, what better time to break the law and probably get away with it?

The mayor met me at the appointed time beside the terminal and explained that we had permission to go onto the ramp once the government aircraft arrived. His Worship was a very conservative man and wanted everything to be perfect, so he took great care in explaining all the proper procedures.

"She is acting as the representative of the Queen, and as such should be given the same respect, which means you must not touch her, don't turn your back to her, and only speak if she speaks to you. You must call her 'Your Honour' or 'Your Worship' and never address her by her name." And he continued prattling on..

As the plane taxied up to the ramp, the gate opened, and I wheeled the big car out to the base of the stairs. I got out and opened the door for the mayor and his wife. The Lieutenant Governor stepped out onto the top step and looked around before starting down the stairs.

The aid decamp, dressed in full military parade uniform complete with white gloves, followed the Lieutenant Governor. As they reached the bottom of the stairs, the mayor bowed, and his wife curtsied. They addressed her as "Your Honour." As they bent down, the Lieutenant Governor glanced over their heads and made eye contact with me.

"Layton?" she blurted, her eyes widening. "Layton? Is that you?" She started to move past the mayor, who was now standing upright again with his mouth gaping open.

"It is, Helen," I replied, smiling as I stepped forward for one of her big hugs. I thought the mayor's eyes would pop out of his head. He had been so intent on instructing me on protocol that I never had a chance to tell him that Helen Hunley had been my Boy Scout leader years before, and she'd been the mayor of our town when my dad served on council.

Helen attended our church, her insurance company had insured my first cars, and she had been our family friend as long as I could remember.

As we cruised out to Beaverlodge, protocol slipped away as Helen and I swapped stories, bringing each other up-to-date on our lives. This delightful encounter reminded me that it is more fun to be with a friend than it is to be someone in the spotlight.

Helen Hunley was the gracious mayor of Rocky Mountain House from 1967 to 1971 and served as MLA and the Province of Alberta's Lieutenant Governor from 1986 to 1991.

12 · Santa and the Happy Hooker

Our old motorhome carved its way through the white blanket that spread before us, undisturbed by other traffic. The full moon peeked quietly through the swirling snow, softly lighting the highway. I navigated using my centreline theory, which is that the road lies equally between the two tall rows of trees. So far, I'd been right.

Myrna was sitting back, her feet up on the wide dashboard, staring out into the darkness in search of her thoughts, which were miles or perhaps years away. She looked as if she did not have a worry, despite the freezing weather and the fact that we might not have been at the end of the world, but on a clearer night we could have seen it from there.

The tranquility of the season seemed to offer a sense of well-being, as did the knowledge that we had three days' heat and water on board and enough food for a week. Still, in just a few more hours, we would be back in the Okanagan, and this weather would be behind us.

The headlights continued searching the night for clues to where the road lay hidden, the motor running faithfully as it had for almost twenty years. Then suddenly, without notice, it experienced massive cardiac arrest, rattled in pain for a few moments, and died.

As we glided silently to a stop, I tried to direct us toward what I thought was the edge of the road. The right wheels found the deeper snow at the shoulder and the old unit groaned to a halt. Then all was quiet, as it should be on Christmas Eve.

Attempts to resuscitate the engine failed, and the realization set in that we were cold, alone, in the dark, and stuck in the middle of nowhere. The snow continued to fall gently, covering us with the same soft blanket as the road, rendering the motorhome almost invisible to any other traffic that might have been following.

I turned on the four-way flashers but was concerned with how long they would last. I knew we had to get off the highway before a large truck ploughed into the back of our unit.

Living in the north had taught us to be prepared, and one of the precautions we had taken was to install an old radiotelephone. Finally, after a number of tries, I connected and was glad to hear her nasal voice:

"Operator."

"This is TJ 76442, operator, and I have a bit of an emergency here."

"Go ahead."

"We are approximately sixteen kilometres north of Blue River and our vehicle has stopped. Can you contact the closest RCMP for us, please?"

"Hang on." And the phone was silent for what seemed like an eternity.

"Blue River RCMP detachment."

I explained our predicament and asked if he could find a tow truck and send it out for us.

"The only tow-truck driver around here always gets drunk Christmas Eve, so even if I knew where to find him, he'd be in no condition to help."

"We can't stay here; I'm sure we'll be hit before morning."

"I might be able to reach a truck from another community, but it'll be expensive."

There seemed to be no other choice, so I told him to do what he could. A short time later our phone rang.It was the tow company, "Happy Hooker," asking us to confirm that we really wanted them to come sixty kilometres on Christmas Eve.

It was just before midnight, about the time jolly old Saint Nick should be appearing, but instead of a sleigh pulled by eight tiny reindeer, the bright flashing lights announced the arrival of a large tow truck.

The driver jumped down and stepped into the light, and we could not believe what we saw, an overweight man with a full white beard and long white hair. Unlike Santa, he kept his hair in a ponytail, and instead of a red suit, he wore a jean jacket with the arms cut off. On second thought, he looked more like a charter member of the Hell's Angels.

Like Santa, he said not a word but went straight to his work, walking around the motorhome and stopping every few seconds to bend down and peer beneath it. After some thought, he crawled underneath and hooked us to the truck. Then he hoisted the front wheels off the ground and told Myrna and I to get into his truck. She sat on the passenger's bucket seat, and I settled down on top of a very cold and hard steel toolbox.

With a jerk, our small procession started out with the headlights following the trail the tow truck had made on the way in, while the flashing yellow light illuminated the trees on both sides of the road.

"I hope we didn't take you away from your family tonight," Myrna said, so grateful that someone would come out on Christmas Eve.

"Nope," he answered shortly. "My wife is having a Christmas party at our house for the people she works with."

"I'm sorry."

"Don't be. They're all teachers. I never liked teachers when I was young, and I don't like them now either."

The tone of his voice seemed to indicate he did not wish to talk, so we let the night fall silent. For hours we bounced down the road, the toolbox becoming harder with every bump. The driver stared ahead through the swirling snow (who knows where his thoughts were?). Then he suddenly spoke as though he was talking to himself.

"I don't believe in Christmas, anyway. Just another damn reason for people to spend all their hard-earned income. I like the fact that you took me away from that party and gave me a chance to make some extra money tonight."

He continued to relay how the world was conspiring against the working guy, especially him. The kilometres melted away, and eventually so did his grumpy disposition.

"Why are you two out here on a night like this?" he asked. "I thought everyone would be sitting by a fire somewhere."

We told him we were keeping up a Christmas tradition of meeting our two daughters at Silver Star Mountain, where we would camp and ski for a week. We would ski the brilliant white snow by day and drink gallons of steaming hot chocolate while we played card games at night.

He finally asked where we wanted to go, but the choices were limited. There were no places in the area to stop, as nothing was open during the holiday season, so we decided to have the motorhome hauled all the way to Kamloops. When we reached Clearwater, our Santa stopped for a change of clothes and a short nap. We spent the balance of Christmas Eve in an alley rocking gently on the tow hook.

No wise men came bearing gifts, no shepherds, no angels, just Myrna and me on a peaceful Christmas Eve. We were reminded of its importance and how another couple was stranded that same night two thousand years before.

Meet the Family—Part Two

Kathy is our eldest. Like her father before her, she thought, "Why waste time getting high marks? If you need 50 percent to pass, then 51 to 55 percent should be adequate." In fact, it's people like Kathy and I who make the top half of the class possible.

This kind of thinking drove Myrna, who was always an honour student, crazy. When she heard about the summer youth university program, where high school students stay in residence at the University of Alberta and choose university programs taught by grad students, she enrolled Kathy.

After her first visit there, Kathy came home excited about how wonderful going to university is. She wanted to know if she could go again the following summer. Myrna explained that it was expensive and perhaps not a good investment, given Kathy's current marks. However, if Kathy would improve her marks, Myrna said she'd reconsider.

Kathy became an A student. As she prepared for her grade-12 finals, I offered to take her on a one-week bike trip through the Gulf and San Juan Islands providing she graduated with good marks. I told her if she did not do well on her finals, I would take her on a two-week bike trip.

I'm not sure if being threatened with riding a bike every day with her dad was the motivation or not, but Kathy graduated an A student and went on to Simon Fraser University to study business and psychology.

Katherine got the last laugh by convincing me she should take an extra business course on the NAFTA agreement. It was only after I agreed that I learned it was only offered the final semester at the University of Mexico.

Today Katherine has Trevor to take her biking and little Nora to ensure I still come to visit.

13 · I Am Dying of Baldness

Our youngest son, Liam, began drum lessons last year and, at age thirteen, plans to become a rock star. He decided that in order to be a drummer, he had to leave his buzz cut behind and begin growing his hair.

He grew the great surfer look of the sixties; in fact, he sort of looks like Dennis Wilson. You remember him, drummer for the Beach Boys. The one who said, "I do not want to shower on the boat. I would prefer to wash up on shore." If you recall, just like Natalie Wood, that is exactly what he did. It was not the career path I had envisioned for my son.

I rallied enough to tell Liam how I wished my hair looked that good. He wanted to know why I didn't just grow it out. I tried to explain how my hair is far too thin and the curls all go in different directions, to which he simply said, "Cool."

I suggested that because his hair is so thick and we share the same DNA, he could donate some hair to fill in my growing bald spot.

His response was quick. "You can have one of my kidneys if you need it, but leave my hair alone."

"What are you saying? You would not donate some hair to your own dad?" I tried to feign disappointment.

"I might if you were dying of baldness, but I've never heard of that happening. And I need my hair. Besides, you already have a woman."

So that is where it stands. Unless I start dying of baldness, Liam is not coming to my rescue.

What is it about turning fifty that causes a man to lose the hair on his head and begin growing it in places that were previously bald?

And why do women find a man with a full head of hair sexy, yet a man with a full ear of hair not? Bushy eyebrows or nose hair are not high on women's lists of preferred male attributes either. I was thinking of letting my eyebrows grow so that as I lose the hair on my head, I can comb my eyebrows back.

I've just read a study that suggests men who still have any of their hair when they die usually still sport the same hairstyle they wore in their youth. That is why we see some white ducktails and grey ponytails on half-bald men, and very thin shoulder-length hair on weathered old faces.

That may be my problem. I looked at a childhood photo and noted I had no hair. In fact, I had no teeth and was wearing a diaper. Is that any indication of where I am headed? I am not getting older; I am regressing. In fact, this may be how I get even with Liam. He may have the hair, but he'll end up stuck babysitting me.

Perhaps God is getting even with women for giving men the apple. First He (or She, depending on your religious preference) waits until a woman plights her troth to a wavy-haired young man. Then God robs the man of his sexy, curly locks and replaces them with wispy, wiry hair growing in the most imaginative places.

A young lady asked Liam to attend the fair with her and her family. As he prepared to go, I handed him the shaving cream and suggested perhaps he should have his first shave. I pointed out that he had two blond hairs on his chin that were approaching a quarter-inch in length. He said he thought she preferred that rugged two-day-beard look even if it had taken him thirteen years to achieve it.

Liam later told the young woman what had transpired, and she told him she liked the look. She thought he looked as though he had the start of a goatee.

I am wondering why, if a thirteen-year-old girl has the ability to look at two blond, almost invisible hairs and visualize a goatee, can't you older women look at a head with two small hairs and at least pretend you see a full head? As we lose our hair, must you lose the magic of your imagination?

This whole hair thing just kills me. Hey, that's it! It's killing me, I am dying of baldness! Liam . . . oh, Liam, where are you?

14 · The Kayak Trip

A trip alone is a great adventure, Myrna said, as she presented me with the gift of a one-week kayaking trip. The local college had organized the trip, which was to be off the west coast of Vancouver Island. Was this gift a conspiracy to cash in on my insurance, I wondered?

The idea seemed exciting at first, but as summer approached, I began to have doubts. I suggested to several of my friends that they should join me, but they laughed and politely declined.

A week before the trip I received a letter listing the food and equipment I'd need for the week. Where will I find a wetsuit, in this small northern community, to fit my six-foot-three inch, 225-pound body?

I read on. A one-burner stove? Watertight packing containers? I would be lucky to find any of those items, and with only a few days left, there was no time to order them from the city. I began to worry about how organized this trip really was.

I called the organizer and asked who else would be on the trip, thinking we might share some of the equipment and the twenty-hour drive to Vancouver Island. He told me that the others were a kayak group from a distant community. Only my kayak partner, a young female college student, was local. Great, I thought, someone with whom I will have nothing in common.

I expressed those concerns to the organizer, who said that if I cancelled, I could not get my money back. He said not to be concerned about upsetting the balance of the group; a teacher friend of his had considered joining us and would be happy to take my spot. I said I would think about it and call back.

I discussed this later in the day with a friend, Bill, who admitted he had tried to register some time ago but the organizer had said the trip was full. "Not so," I said, and told him of the conversation concerning the possible newcomer.

"I'll call again," he said. I felt relieved. I did not want to donate the cost of the trip to a stranger, but I worried about struggling to keep up with a group of young jocks wanting to race between islands.

Suppose that an hour into the trip, I discovered I did not want to continue? It's not as though I could catch a whale home. In addition, how would my wife feel when I told her my paddling partner was to be a twenty-something young woman? Bill and I could go at our own pace and create our own adventure. I relaxed and became excited again.

The following night, Bill called to say the organizer had rudely reminded him that he'd already told Bill he could not join the group. I was on edge again. It was time to put an end to this worry.

"I'm going to the college in the morning to demand my money back," I told Myrna as I got into bed that night. "This is crazy. They don't tell you who is on the trip, they give the equipment list out a week before leaving, and everyone is expected to take their own food and stoves, rather than having common supplies. I don't like the sounds of this, so I've decided I'm not going." I was getting tense.

Myrna knows I do not like confrontations and that I would worry about it most of the night. She also has a strong sense of faith. "Relax," she said. "I'll say a prayer for you." She closed her eyes and said a short prayer asking that this be resolved for me. I felt a little better, and we fell asleep.

The next morning I walked into the extension office and asked politely but firmly to speak to the registrar. "I'm sorry, but she's not in. May I help you?" the young woman asked.

"I wish to discuss the kayak trip scheduled for this week."

"Oh, you've heard?" the young lady replied.

"Heard? Heard what?" I asked.

"There was an accident last night. One of the kayaks fell on the organizer while he was loading them. He sprained his wrist. He can't possibly go now, so the trip will have to be postponed for a couple of weeks."

"My summer holidays are scheduled for next week, and I can't change them now," I replied confidently, seeing a better way out.

"We expected that," the young woman sighed. "We are prepared to offer a full refund."

"That'll be fine," I said.

As I drove from the parking lot, an approaching van turned the corner, pulling a trailer full of kayaks. A scowling driver supported a bandaged hand and forearm on the open window. As we passed, I smiled and waved.

He should thank God Myrna did not pray any harder, I thought, or that poor guy might have been killed.

15 · I Am Not Dave Barry

Fred called the other day to say he likes my column and suggested I must be the Canadian Dave Barry. Funny, no one calls Stompin' Tom the "Canadian Garth Brooks" or Celine Dion the "Canadian Madonna." Why not Dave Barry the "American Layton Park?"

I began listing the differences between us, and soon had compiled the opposite of the Kennedy and Lincoln comparison list. You remember them; one was killed in the Ford theatre, the other in a Ford Lincoln. They both had vice presidents named Johnson and both have the same number of letters in their names, and so on.

Well, *Barry* is a five-letter word and *Park* has four. I grant you we both have humour columns, but according to Dave's website, he appears weekly in only 500 newspapers across North America, while according to the editor of *North of Fifty* (circ. 14,000), I am now in fourteen thousand newspapers every month, all here in the Okanagan.

Dave is on the speaking circuit for $30,000 per engagement plus expenses, and then only if he can fit it into his schedule. I, on the other hand, can come over to your place tonight and speak if afterwards you will provide a meal.

Dave studied English at university where he crafted his style; I was expelled from university because of my English. Dave won the coveted Pulitzer Prize; I once won a prize in a Pilsner drinking contest.

I have been to Florida (Dave is from Miami) twice, and I would bet he has never been to B.C.'s Okanagan. The differences are endless. However, I do admit I was just a little pleased at my friend's comment.

I discovered Dave Barry only a couple of years ago, but it was similar to Columbus's discovery of North America. Millions of other people already knew of the existence of each, but that did not count until Columbus and I made our own discoveries.

I first found Dave Barry in the humour section of the bookstore. I was trying to console myself by searching for something funny about turning fifty, when I came across his book on the very subject. I was later surprised to discover that a local paper carried his column, and although I had been writing my short stories only for a select group of warped-minded friends, it inspired me to send them off to a publisher.

With only a minimum amount of begging and extortion, I soon landed my own column. My editor complimented me by saying I had a very creative style, which is a nice way of saying I would still flunk English, but similar warped-minded people might enjoy my writing.

I began to think it was time to bring this question of comparisons to a head and get Dave to leave the comforts of Miami and come to the Okanagan. A community such as Armstrong, I mused, could invite him to their annual fair, where he could defend his title as King of the Humour Columnists by meeting me in a challenge write-a-thon. But someone pointed out that once we converted his fee to Canadian dollars, everyone in town would have to second-mortgage their homes in order to afford his ticket price.

Then I remembered a column he wrote about his paper sending him to New York to defend the honour of Miami after the *Times* ran an unfavourable article about the city. Canadians are too polite to actually write a nasty article about any place, even Miami, in order to attract that type of response, but still the idea has merit.

What do you think? Is there a way a Canadian country boy could entice the big American city boy to visit or at least write about the Okanagan? We know there are a number of reasons his readers would be interested.

For example, Miami has more French-Canadian residents than Montreal and several times more than B.C. Not that there is anything wrong with being a French-Canadian, but we in the West are happy with this arrangement. Suppose that the people of Miami knew that the Kelowna was farther from Montreal (4,707 kilometres) than they are (2,450 kilometres); would that make the Okanagan more attractive?

If his newspaper had enough positive reasons, would they send Dave Barry here? Could we impress Dave so that he wants to come, explore, and accept a challenge to write about our region?

In the meantime, if we can't afford to hire him to come here, if we are too polite to challenge him and too proud to plead with him, then perhaps we will not see his column shed humour and light on our part of the world. However, you still have me, the "Canadian Dave Barry," who promises to continue to bring the Okanagan's important issues to the surface, such as should men be allowed to shop for groceries?

16 · Ode to Sneaky Pete

(and Great Teachers Everywhere)

"You can't call him Sneaky Pete! That is so disrespectful!"

My mother was horrified when I told her the title of this article I wanted to write about one of the teachers from my hometown, after I learned of his failing health. "You should address him as Mr. Feschuck," she admonished me.

Peter taught me in several grades, and I have a hard time believing that was forty years ago. I knew Peter was living in the area but never took the time to seek him out and tell him the things I have been telling others for years. I don't know why I did not take the time to tell him earlier; perhaps it is because I still have some overdue assignments. They were from the current affairs course when he assigned them, and now they are part of the Canadian history program. Mr. Feschuck taught both subjects.

Mr. Feschuck was his name back then, too, but everyone knew him as Sneaky Pete because of the Hush Puppy shoes that allowed him to walk the corridors undetected. As soon as a friend had convinced me to do something I should not, and it always was someone else's fault (honest, Mom), there he was. I was not a bad student, but if it were not for teachers like Peter Feschuck, I might have become one. Pete was not one of the loud or threatening teachers; his technique was more in the manner of guilt intimidation if you were out of line. That may have been where the term "thunderous silence" came from.

When I talked to some of my friends about our school years, we agreed three teachers stick out in our minds, and you can tell by my writing that the English teacher is not one of them. The list included Sneaky Pete, Battle-Axe Bert, and Miserable Mike.

Battle-Axe was the name for a crusty woman who seemed old, although now in my adult mind I realize she must have been only about forty at the time. She loved to carry a yardstick and could slap it across the top of the desk with such force that it would shatter every eardrum within fifty metres. She then turned an icy stare in the offender's direction. There was no need for further discussion as everyone froze to the spot.

I talked to Mrs. Bert once about how she felt about people calling her Battle-Axe, although no one dared to call any of these teachers by their underground monikers. They not only knew what they were, but I think they were proud of them.

Battle-Axe said she thought of it as a badge of honour. A badge she had earned because the students said it with a certain amount of respect. It was tough love before someone coined the phrase.

Miserable Mike was my math and biology teacher, whose loud voice and ominous presence scared me for a while. It was a tough persona that he carefully cultivated to keep students in their place. I know that to be the case because after class, he dedicated hours to coaching hockey, and I saw a different side of the man.

What these three teachers had in common was that they truly cared about their students. Some of the ruffians who tried hard to torment these good people are now schoolteachers and principals themselves. Others are engineers, accountants, business people, successful farmers, and pillars of their communities.

This is what outstanding teachers like Peter Feschuck leave as their legacy. They look upon their careers as a profession. They see their duty to mould and shape the generations of tomorrow by making students accountable.

With the advantage of hindsight, as I look at my peers who were taught by Peter, I would have to say he did a pretty good job. Teachers like Peter do not demand respect, they earn it. When students referred to him as Sneaky Pete, it was with an air of respect like that commanded by the sergeant majors of yesterday. Students knew there was a line to toe at the same time they knew they could count on these teachers anytime they needed help.

Like Battle-Axe, Sneaky Pete's nickname was a badge of honour. So it is with the utmost respect that I dedicate this story to him, as he was largely responsible for me continuing my education. On account of him, I developed a keen interest in current affairs and developed a deep desire to study and write about history.

I knew he would not allow us students to get away with things, not because he was mean-spirited or a rule enforcer, but because he truly cared for us. So excuse me, Mom, but I don't think it is disrespectful to say thanks, Sneaky Pete!

Peter Feschuck passed away on May 27, 2004 and they read this story at his funeral. Since that time I have had a number of his old students tell me how much he influenced their lives as well. I know there are countless other teachers out there changing young lives for the better daily and without recognition. Next time you think about it, why not call one of your old teachers and thank them.

17 · The Autopsy

"Hello. May I speak to the doctor?" the woman panted, choking back panic, then added without waiting for an answer, "It's an emergency!"

My friend has a veterinarian practice that includes seeing all types of exotic birds and animals. The receptionist put the following call through to him.

"Hello, how can I help you?" he asked.

"Doctor," she began, after identifying herself, "our budgie just died. May I bring it in this morning so can you perform an autopsy?"

"You want an autopsy on your budgie?" he repeated, not sure, he had heard her correctly.

"Yes. I'm just loading the kids in the van so I can take them to school. I could bring it in right away." The sound of her voice indicated she was in a hurry.

"I'm sorry," he said, "but I don't have the equipment to do an autopsy on a small bird. I could send it to Vancouver, but it would be very expensive, and it probably died from any one of a hundred natural causes."

"That's okay. I don't mind paying! I'm worried it might be from some disease that could infect our other pets, so it's important that we know. Can I drop it off on the way to school?"

"If you insist, that'll be fine. I'll look at it right away," he answered.

A few minutes later, the woman rushed through the front door of the office and dropped a small brown bag on the reception counter. "Will you see that the doctor gets this for me?" Without waiting for an answer, she flew back out the door and disappeared as quickly as she had come.

Shortly after lunch, the receptionist came into the Vet's office and announced rather sheepishly that she had forgotten to give him the bag earlier in the day. He explained it was a dead budgie and assured her, the couple of hours that had elapsed would not make any difference to the bird.

Taking the bag from her, he opened it and peered inside. A look of concern fell over his face. He reached inside with cupped hands wondering aloud if he had acted sooner might he have saved a small child from a traumatic experience.

Then carefully he removed his hand and in it was a ham sandwich, while somewhere, a child opened his lunch bag amidst his friends and withdrew his dead pet budgie.

Meet the Family—Part Three

When Carson was about five years old, Myrna was driving him home from kindergarten when he looked up and asked, "Mom, what are bitches?"

Trying to keep her composure (after all, he was in Catholic French-immersion kindergarten), she said calmly, "Well, do you remember Purdy from '101 Dalmatians'?"

"Yes."

"Well, Purdy was a female dog, and that is what a bitch is. Sometimes people call other people that as a rude comment, but you should never do that. It is not a nice word."

"Oh."

"Where did you hear that word, Carson?"

"From my teacher," he answered nonchalantly.

"What!" she screamed in her head. Catholic French-immersion kindergarten! He should not be hearing those kinds of words at school. She calmly continued, "So, how did she use the word?"

"She read us a story about a boy who had a prickle in his bitches," he replied.

Great, she thought. I have just taught our son a bad word. Then she added aloud, "Britches. Britches. You can forget that other word; britches is a good word."

18 · Oh, Bobby!

Growing up with three sisters meant that during the inevitable sibling disputes, it was usually me alone against them. They would find ways to make me angry, and I would retaliate by finding a way to trick or surprise them.

When we were older we got along very well, but I still liked to pull the occasional prank, so when my sister Pat was about to turn forty, I tried to think of something I could do for, or should I say, *to* her. Then it came to me.

Do you remember Bobby Curtola? He was one of the good-looking young singers of the early sixties; his big hit was "Fortune Teller." Pat was a big fan of Bobby's. She had once attended a concert of his, where Bobby handed her a bottle of Coke from the stage.

This was to be one of the biggest treasures of her life. I, on the other hand, was not a Bobby Curtola fan and had little respect for this treasure. I kidnapped it a couple of times and would tell her it was lost, or replace it with an empty bottle and tell her I drank it. Of course that would make her cry, so I would return it to its place of honour, in the center of Pat's dresser.

When Pat left home, the bottle remained in her old room for years. Then tragedy struck. Dad and Mom moved and someone threw the bottle out. Pat never forgot and mentioned it when we would get together, thinking I must have had something to do with its disappearance.

That's what made this idea so great. I discovered B.C. Coke producers had a promotion going in which they were bottling their pop in the old-style bottles. I went to Dawson Creek and bought one. I knew a friend of ours, Don Lindsay, who had worked with Bobby, so I called him and asked if he could get Bobby to sign the bottle and a card for her. No problem, he promised.

Next, Myrna and I invited Pat to join us at the Edmonton Inn for a long lunch. I phoned the inn and asked if they could reserve a private area in the restaurant for a small birthday party. As we were preparing to leave Grande Prairie, the mechanic found our airplane had a problem and we were a half an hour late getting off. Myrna and I arrived at the Inn ten minutes past noon and could not find Pat.

Finally we asked the cashier, who had misinterpreted our request and had seated Pat in a large private dining room. As Myrna and I entered the room, Pat was sitting alone in a sea of empty tables and chairs. She asked nervously why we had reserved such a large space for lunch.

As I was busy explaining what had happened, Don walked up behind us, introduced himself, and said, "I'd like to introduce you to Bobby Curtola."

You can imagine Pat's surprise when Bobby walked in, singing "Happy Birthday"! He presented the new bottle of Coke, then swept her over backward and gave her a kiss. He began singing some of his songs unaccompanied and danced around the floor with her.

Bobby joined us for a lunch that lasted the better part of the afternoon. Once again, I succeeded in making my sister cry over a bottle of Coke. Now, what can I dream up for the other two sisters?

I tried to find a good photo of my three sisters to share with you but every time a camera came out they posed as above, afraid I might use the photo somehow . . . well guess who gets the last laugh? I love the photo!

19 · Memories

"That reminds me of a story," my father said. "It's about what's-his-name . . . the fellow who lived north of us in Leslieville."

"Jim Brown?" said Uncle Arlan quickly.

"No, not Jim. This guy farmed just north of the river."

"I know who you mean," added Uncle Howard. "He had the old McCormick tractor, what was his name?"

"No, not the guy with the McCormick. This fellow had a three-wheel John Deere," Dad responded. "He lived about a mile north of the guy with the McCormick."

"Oh, yeah!" Arlan answered. "Now I know who you mean. He walked with a limp."

"No, that was his brother," Howard added. "*I* know who you mean. What was his name?"

"You don't mean Fred Johnson?" asked Arlan, furrowing his brow.

"No, not Fred. It was his brother, John." Dad leaned back, smiling at his two brothers with a look of satisfaction. It had been over sixty years since they had lived there, yet with some prompting they had remembered a neighbour they probably hadn't thought about in as long.

"So, what about him?" Wes looked at Dad with curiosity.

"What do you mean, what about him?" Dad sat up.

"You said you were reminded of a story about him," Arlan said.

"I did?" Dad hesitated. "I don't remember what it was."

The conversation went something like that the last time these three brothers got together at a family reunion. Two of Dad's brothers passed away shortly after, and it made me realize how little I knew about my father. That motivated me to record some of his stories before his own passing so I could preserve them for my kids.

Nothing provokes more laughter or induces more fear than the loss of memory. Perhaps it's because to one degree or another we are all subject to some memory loss as we age. I saw Dad struggle with frustration over his memory loss, and then, as I approached fifty, I began noticing a loss of my own memory.

Forgetting a friend's name is embarrassing; so is trying to remember why you came downstairs. Memory is a funny thing. I can't remember where or when I am supposed to pick up my wife, but I can still remember most of the words for many of the hit songs from the sixties.

I still remember the smell of dirt mixed with hydraulic oil that filled my Grandpa's shop on the farm. And the smell of Grandma's baking bread filling the kitchen, mmm. Yet, despite how easily I recall these childhood images, today I struggle to remember whether it is Wednesday or Friday.

"What will our kids remember?" I asked Myrna.

"They'll think of me every time they see a red convertible because I always tease them that that's what I could have had,if not for their braces. Now they point them out and call them 'Mom's car,'" she answered.

If you want to do something special for your children and grandchildren, I encourage you to begin recording a few your own memories for them to enjoy.

That reminds me of a story about . . . what was his name?

Meet the Family—Part 4

When we were preparing for Mom and Dad's fiftieth anniversary, we asked the grandchildren to make them a card. This was what my son Liam wrote:
How to stay married for 50 years
By Liam Park (age 8)

Love each other for a long time.

Marry and never divorce.

When it is their birthday, get them a present they would love.

At Christmas, help each other decorate.

Agree on inviting the same people to a party.

20 · Vacuuming Sucks

Vacuums suck, or at least they are supposed to. Ours no longer did, so after we moved and renovated the house, I went shopping for a new one. What I found was confusing, and I hope my experience will assist you should you ever need to buy a new vacuum.

The standard upright basic model is easy to store and costs about $150 at most chain stores, but before buying, I thought I should look around first. Once you commit to shopping for a vacuum, a news bulletin goes out to all the salespeople within five hundred kilometres giving them your name, phone number, address, and financial net worth statement.

At one point, salespeople were lining up at the door. I had so many free demonstrations on our area rugs that I can't remember them all, but I do recall that each salesperson found more dirt in them than the last. I began to worry that after one more demonstration, all the fibre would be sucked right out of the carpet.

It seems there are hundreds of models and each one has improvements over the last. The prices start a little lower than a small Mercedes, but the vacuum weighs slightly more so you know you're getting a good deal.

Several come with twin, high—and low-beam headlights, a three-speed transmission, and reverse. I asked for the all-wheel-drive units, but they will not be out until next year.

One type is filled with water and looks like the robot from Star Wars, R2-D2. It follows you around the house babbling as it bumps into furniture.

The last pair of young salespeople finally appeared. They were wound up like three-dollar watches and said that their machine was such a good investment they were going to buy one as well. They then added that first they had to make a couple of sales so they could leave home and rent a place to live so they would have something to vacuum.

To illustrate the investment side of the opportunity, they showed how their unit compared in cost over a twenty-year period to buying several cheaper models that would only last a few years each and have to be replaced with escalating dollars. I could make additional money from the referral fees I would receive for giving out names of friends whom I would like to see profit from the same sort of investment.

By the time they had finished, they'd drawn up a page of figures that my financial planner would have been impressed with. The enthusiasm during their presentation was so high that I felt guilty for saying no. I watched their deflated and dejected looks as they trudged down the walk, their unit and sales kit in tow as they headed back home to Mom.

I settled on the built-in model and ran lines all through the house; this way, I needed only the short hose. I even installed the automatic dustpan under the kitchen cupboard. Once the dirt was swept to within a foot of the baseboard, it suddenly disappeared.

That's how I got the idea I could install a grate over the entire floor then duct it to a thirty-inch wall fan, ensuring I would never have to sweep or push hoses around again. Just one flick of the switch and the entire floor would be sucked clean. If I used the forty-eight-inch fan, it could also double as a downdraft range hood, but that idea never occurred to me until the built-in was in place.

You would think my buddy Gavin, being a contractor, would have done the same, but he didn't. However, he did confess to the following two incidents.

The first was New Year's Eve. While helping his wife with the cleaning, he accidentally sucked up one of her scarves. He had to pull apart the pipes from his built-in to dig it out, and then managed to shake the dust out and put the scarf back in the bedroom before she discovered it was missing.

Had it not been for her overhearing the story while at a party, she might never have known. What she did not hear about, however, was the time he accidentally sucked up one of her socks. He did not want to go through the dismantling job again so he quickly looked around, then got rid of the evidence by sucking up the other one.

It is at times like these that a man needs a good vacuum and one that really sucks.

21 · Parasailing

Like most pilots, I have never been attracted to parachuting. We believe no one in their right mind should jump out of a perfectly good airplane.

However, one summer several years ago, I was lying on a beach watching the first parasailers I had ever seen drifting lazily up and down Mara Lake. That looks like an adventure, I thought. They weren't jumping out of airplanes; boats were just towing them along. After watching them go back and forth for a day and a half without incident, I thought I had to give this a try.

I walked over to the young fellow who appeared to be the organizer and asked what it would cost to go for a ride. The price was reasonable, and he said there was just one spot left at 6 p.m. the next day. I agreed to take it and returned to watch the following afternoon, which also passed without incident.

One by one, people would get into the harness on the beach and take two or three steps. Then, before anyone reached the water's edge, they would head skyward like homesick angels. As my time came closer, I began getting excited.

Finally, it was my turn. A beach boy who was too well-tanned trussed me up in the harness and gave me a handful of ropes. I asked what I needed to know.

"Can you run?" he asked. When I assured him I could, he said, "When I yell 'run,' you run. Don't worry about all the lines. Don't pull any of them or try to steer. Just run and enjoy."

What I did not know was they had bought the boat only two days earlier and had not yet towed anyone my size. Standing on the beach with a couple of men holding up the parachute behind me, I waited with anticipation as the boat motor gunned and the command came, "Go!"

Down the beach I ran, both feet still solidly hitting the ground when I reached the water. I tried to keep running but it became difficult as the water became deeper. Once past my knees, I could no longer lift my feet out of the lake, fell forward and was dragged across the top of the water. Just before I drank half the lake and drowned, I was suddenly airborne. What a feeling! Looking down between my dripping legs, I could see the boat a hundred metres below.

The plan was to go up the east side of the lake to the north end then turn around and come back down the west side. By the time we reached the lake's north end, the wind had come up and whitecaps were forming. The boat turned west, but the parachute still faced north into the wind, tracking along on the south side of the boat.

The wind was too strong and my chute would not turn and follow the boat. They turned the boat to face east but the results were the same, the wind kept me facing north.

Finally, the driver decided the wind was too strong to continue. He could not turn around so he cut the engine, but the parachute did not descend and instead began pulling the boat backward into the waves.

The 350-foot rope was tied to the ski bar in the middle of the boat, and as the parachute pulled the boat back, the vessel began to go under the waves. More waves lapped up over the back, and as more of the boat was flooded, its nose rose out of the water. I watched as the boat capsized, its two occupants diving wildly over the side.

I had a great view of the event, but was not terribly excited about what I was witnessing. The thought that kept bothering me was what if the boat sinks and the lake is deeper than three hundred and fifty feet? I'm not sure how to get out of this rig, and if the lake is deeper than the length of the rope, I have a problem.

The parachute still did not come down. Instead, it became more like a kite. It began pulling the boat backward through the chop. It would be a good time to know what string to pull, I thought, but it is a helluva time to start experimenting.

Several boats came to the rescue of my boat's drivers. An off-duty member of the airborne beach patrol, driving a large boat, reached the swimmers first and pulled them aboard. They hooked the rope that secured me to the boat under a tie-down bracket on the side of the rescue boat and began driving up the line, bringing the parachute closer to the water.

Eventually I was dunked into the water, but the chute stayed inflated. The wind would catch it again and drag me across the top of the water in a large arc, and then it would dunk me again. Back and forth it dragged and dunked me.

When the rescue boat finally reached me, the driver grabbed the front shroud lines and yanked them down around my head and neck. I threw them off, concerned that if the chute took off again, it would choke me, but his actions collapsed the chute. Finally, the driver pulled me aboard.

"What were you doing?" he yelled at me. "Why didn't you just pull on the front lines and bring yourself down?" Before I could answer, he began yelling at the two boat owners. "And why didn't you just let the quick release go?"

"We were afraid he would take off with our chute," the tall one replied. "We just bought this outfit and we didn't know what to do." His companion nodded in dumb agreement.

All ended well, and I learned jumping out of a perfectly good airplane is not the only bad idea one can have that involves a parachute.

Meet the Family—Part 4—this should be your first one because it introduces the concept—so make this part 1

It seemed a shame to waste the extra pages where a story doesn't finish on the right side of the page, so I thought it would be a good idea to use these pages throughout the book to introduce you to members of my family and share some of their funny stories.

In the fall of 1996 while I was away, Myrna was invited, as the president of the Grande Prairie Real Estate Board, to attend a supper with the premier of the province, Ralph Klein. She felt it was an honour and accepted.

The boys (six and four) weren't used to Mom going out alone when Dad was away, and they began questioning where she was going off to.

Myrna found it difficult to explain who the premier was, so she asked if they knew who the kings were in their storybooks. They said they did.

"The Premier is sort of like the king of Alberta," she explained, "and I'm going to a supper with a lot of other people to welcome him to our town." The boys were impressed and satisfied, so they granted their approval.

Later that night Myrna had an opportunity to tell the story to "Ralph," who thought it amusing. In a demonstration of how laid-back he really was, he took the time to write a note to the boys on the back of the program invitation. At the bottom he signed, "from King Ralph . . . (Klein) . . . Premier of Alberta."

I am of the opinion that any kids who are on a first-name basis with a King should be listened to. Perhaps they have lessons for all of us. Thus I began recording some of their more philosophical comments and stories.

Meet the Family—Part Five

Like most mothers, Myrna has developed highly acute hearing when it comes to listening to little voices talking in the rear seat.

As we drove down the road one day, she suddenly sat up straight and turned around to face our six-year-old son, Carson.

"What did you say?"

"Nothing, Mom," he answered nervously.

"Yes, you did. I heard you," said Myrna. "What did you say?"

"I didn't say anything." Carson fidgeted in his seat.

Turning to three-year-old Liam, the weak link, Myrna continued. "What did your brother just say?"

Liam sat up straight, took a deep breath, and with the utmost pride, said, "Carson says that our name spelled backward is SH**," clearly enunciating the swear word.

"Close," Myrna laughed. "It's KRAP. And by the way, Liam, your name spelled backward is KRAP MAIL."

22 · The Music Promoter

"Why not get into the music promotion business?" Don Lindsay asked. "The radio station says Leroy Van Dyke, 'The Auctioneer,' is available for a series of concerts after the New Year. As the promoter, your company would get a lot of free publicity, and you would make a profit."

Don was our advertising account manager at the local radio station. He was well aware of how much money our construction company was spending on marketing.

Having never been in the promotion business, I thought it sounded like an easy way to cover some of those advertising expenses, and any additional money made would be a welcome bonus.

The only hiccup was a $10,000 guarantee to the singer. How big a risk can that be, I thought? With three venues, it's only $3,500 in sales per location plus expenses. At $25 per ticket, it would take fewer than 250 tickets per location to make money. We were in.

The first location in Dawson Creek, B.C., presented the first obstacles. Unfortunately, we did not factor in the kind of weather that can and did come in January. Forty below and a month after Christmas, when most bank accounts are trying to recover from over-exertion, was reason enough for people to stay away in droves and it was financial disaster.

"Don't worry," Don said. "Grande Prairie will be strong and Grande Cache is a country town. We'll do great there." He sounded confident, and he was right. Despite cold weather, about 350 people turned out in Grande Prairie.

The next day the road crew loaded the humpback Greyhound tour bus, as Don and I piled into my pick-up and led the way down Highway 40. "Highway" is being generous; it was a dirt forestry road that ran parallel to the Rocky Mountains almost the full length of the province. The primary use of the road was for hunting, fishing, and fighting forest fires. It was also the shortest route to Grande Cache, about two hundred kilometres away.

The road passed over what was known as the Smokey Tower Hill, at the top of which sat a ranger station. Besides being long and steep, the road had a twist at the bottom, preventing vehicles from taking a run at it to build up speed.

Three times the old bus had tried to make the hill, and three times either the tires spun out or the bus powered out before reaching the crest. Then we would back it up a half mile to make another attempt.

Watching as Leroy put the chains on by himself, I said, "With a chain on only one wheel, it won't have enough traction. Do you have any more chains?"

"Nope, only need one chain in Tennessee," Leroy answered flatly as he looked up. His guitar player, standing with his hands in his pockets, drawled, "I'd give you a hand, Leroy, but lately everything I touch just turns to shee-et."

I remembered seeing a tanker truck earlier, parked at an oilrig about three or four kilometres back, so I drove my pickup back to see if I could solicit his help. The trucker looked at me as though I must be out of my mind as I explained our predicament.

"You have a bus where?" he said incredulously. Finally, he said he had to wait awhile to load, so he would drop his pup trailer and give us a pull.

Back at the bus, the trucker hooked it up to a chain and asked what kind of transmission it had. "Two-speed," replied Leroy.

Shaking his cowboy hat from side to side at that answer, the trucker walked back to his rig. "Put that bus in high gear and hang on," he said as he crawled into the cab. He turned to me and said, "You go to the top of the Smokey and stop anyone from coming down. We'll be using the whole road."

Black smoke was screaming from the twin stacks as the truck came over the crest, the bus's front wheels barely touching the ground.

After the trucker unhooked his truck and refused the money we offered, Leroy asked if he was a country fan. Posing that question to a northern trucker is the equivalent of asking a cowboy if he likes horses. With a look of half-disgust, the trucker said, "'Course I am. I keep a real collection of tapes in the truck?"

"Wait here," replied Leroy as he disappeared into the bus. Returning a minute later with his hands full of tapes and albums, he handed them to the bewildered trucker who suddenly recognized the face on the cover. "You're Leroy Van Dyke? Well, I'll be!" he exclaimed, pumping Leroy's hand. "I'm really pleased to meet you. Who's going to believe I met The Auctioneer halfway down Highway 40?"

A few more handshakes and he left smiling and shaking his head as he clung to his new treasures. It took ten hours on the road to go one hundred kilometres, and the tired crew just in time to set up for the show.

The turnout in Grande Cache was worse than Dawson Creek. I finally went to the bar and gave away tickets just to have some bodies in the room. After the show, we all went to the hotel restaurant for supper. The singer in the adjoining lounge announced the great Leroy Van Dyke was in the next room and maybe if they clapped loud enough he would join them for a few songs.

Leroy said that he would not expect a mechanic in the crowd to come out and fix his bus free. He explained that he made his living singing and I was trying to make one promoting his concerts, so it wouldn't make economic sense for him to perform for free. He asked me to go and thank them, but he would have to decline. The audience broke into applause as I walked into the room, only to be disappointed when they realized I was not Leroy.

With well under a hundred paid tickets in Grande Cache, the net outcome of three venues was grim. We shook hands as Leroy loaded his crew into the bus and headed south, non-stop for Tennessee. Don and I got back in the pickup and headed home. I vowed to pay for my advertising in future and not be tempted into promoting another "easy money" venture.

23 · The King and I

The music "Odyssey 2000" began, the volume filling the room. Bright, coloured lights began to sweep the crowd, bringing it to life.

The crowd jumped to their feet, clapping wildly as four bodyguards escorted in the tall, slightly heavy, middle-aged singer. The full black jumpsuit, gold sequins dancing in the lights, a wide white belt with a pattern of studs and jewels, and his jet-black hair combed back just above the chrome-framed sunglasses, all spelled Elvis. The music continued to build and the pace quickened until the procession reached the stage.

The four bodyguards, all dressed in bright red western shirts, blue jeans, sunglasses, and western hats, positioned themselves at the front, between the stage and the audience. Jumping onto the stage, the singer grabbed a guitar with a wide white studded strap matching his belt as the band, Apple Jack, became louder and faster, bringing the music to a crescendo.

Women near the front began throwing their underwear on stage as the excitement continued to build to a frenzy. The three hundred realtors in the ballroom of the Jasper Park Lodge were on their feet, clapping and screaming. The King grabbed the mike and began belting out:

"Since my baby left me,
I have a house to sell,
Down at the end of Lonely Street . . ."
The song ended, but not the music, as they broke into:
"Return to Vendor,
This just won't do,
Drapes aren't included,
What should I do?"
And, "You ain't nothing but a *realtor*."
The crowd went wild right up to the announcement, "Elvis has left the building."

It all began in the strangest way. The Grande Prairie Real Estate Board was to provide entertainment for the annual Alberta Real Estate Association's convention. While sitting around the table planning it, someone suggested an Elvis impersonator should be in the show, along with a number of other events.

One of the fellows and I began singing some Elvis songs, substituting real estate words. We soon had five or six numbers that would work. After some refinement, the songs were ready. At some point, possibly between beer five and ten, a volunteer had persuaded me to become the King. At the time, it seemed like such a good idea.

We gathered for weekly rehearsals, but the King was too shy and could not stand up in front of his peers. The other acts were getting better and the show was really taking shape, but everyone was worried about the Elvis act.

The closer it got to show time, the more nervous Elvis became, uttering secret prayers for assistance in finding a way out. The volunteer began to approach other board members to see if someone else would take it on. Most said he would do a great job, gave him a pat on the back, then walked away laughing. Elvis felt the situation was desperate, yet he could not rehearse. Finally, the show weekend loomed.

The night before the show, the acts did a dress rehearsal, which was outstanding, but the King did not appear. In fact, there were fewer reported sightings of him than the real Elvis. The following day no one saw him. This was perhaps the only weekend *The National Enquirer* did not report a sighting.

"A half hour to show time. Are you ready?" the producer asked over the phone.

The reply was a feeble "Yes."

"Are you sure of all your lines?" he continued, which was followed by an even weaker reply.

"Have you been practising on your own?" He was again assured that this was the case, although it did not sound as convincing as it should have. "I am concerned I might forget the words," the King confessed.

"Don't worry," the producer replied. "I've already written all the words down on large sheets of paper and taped them to the floor of the stage. No one in the audience can see them, but they're large enough that you'll be able to." He went on to say that the band had arrived and practised. Elvis silently prayed to let him change places with the real Elvis, wherever he might be.

The wife and another woman came to the rescue, carrying a tray of drinks known as the Caesar: vodka, Tabasco sauce, Worcestershire sauce, celery salt, Clamato juice, and a stick of celery, just to make them healthy. They taste marvellous and slide down so easily. I learned to reject them a long time ago, especially if I planned to stand up in the immediate future, but on this day I did not protest.

The two women insisted that the drinks were only for medicinal purposes. "They'll make you relax and loosen up." They claimed the King himself had used them for relaxing from time to time.

"That's why he is no longer with us!" the King replied, but they ignored his comment.

After two of these drinks, I agreed to get dressed. But this Elvis said he still did not think he could go through with the show.

"After all," he reminded Myrna, "I haven't even practised."

"Oh, don't worry about it," she said, offering him another Caesar. "Everyone is here for fun; no one is going to be critical of your performance."

"Very easy for you to say, all you have to do is get the crowd going wild, throwing panties and screaming," he answered, swallowing the drink.

One more Caesar as they finished dyeing his hair black. Another drink and he let them add the belt and scarf. One more, and he began swaggering down the hall as if he really were the King. Standing outside of the back entrance to the ballroom, he thought, they have gone to a lot of work to get one nervous performer ready to go.

We could hear the announcement, "Ladies and gentlemen, let me introduce the star of tonight's show, Mr. Elvis Present-an-offer-ly." Elvis's entrance music and the applause became deafening as the door opened. The producer was standing just inside; he looked at me and said, "How's Elvis doing?"

"Perfect," I replied, walking past him and surrounded by my four bodyguards. And the rest, as they say, is history.

The show was an outstanding success. My adrenaline was pumping so hard, the crowd was so responsive, and I was having so much fun that I did not want to stop. I may have continued had several women, led by the wife, not started rushing the stage. The bodyguards held them back, as planned, just like an Elvis show; however, the acting of these women was so convincing that it induced several other women in the audience to join them.

As quickly as it had begun, it ended. I jumped from the stage and ran out the rear door and back into obscurity. I now understand the incredible rush performers get and why so many have drinking problems.

One of three Whales playing in front of Salty Towers
If you tell Neil and Maggy that you don't know me you might
get a better rate!

24 · Sooke and the Ice Floes

Lately, I have been waking up feeling a little stiffer and sorer than usual. This reminded me of my increasing age, and I began to wonder when my family would follow the great Canadian custom and set me adrift on an ice floe.

I decided to minimize the risk by leaving the Great White North and moving to Kelowna, B.C., where the lake never freezes. Furthermore, I refuse to leave the Okanagan Valley during winter.

But recently we took a winter break and decided to visit a bed and breakfast at Sooke on Vancouver Island. A quick check of the Internet told me there were no ice floes there, so I agreed to go.

I used to wonder what heaven was like. I used to think it was somewhere in the sky, where St. Peter, dressed in a white robe with long white hair and matching beard, would greet new arrivals at the gate.

Heaven is often portrayed as a place where one drifts around on a cloud, eating some brand of cream cheese.

But I now know heaven is really located in Sooke, where guests are met at the gate of Salty Towers by a slightly greying, misplaced prairie boy named Neil Flynn and his golden Lab, Salty.

Seeing an Irishman in heaven relieved one of my worries, and the thought of drifting around the West Coast in Neil's fishing boat eating smoked salmon and cream cheese on a bagel gave me something to look forward to.

At the risk of sounding like a fisherman, which I am not, I will tell you we spent a day pulling in salmon so fast that my arm got tired from reeling. Neil was often running between the three rods, lowering the downriggers on one while the other two were being reeled in with fish on the line.

Neil said it's not like that all the time, but I believe he may tell everyone that so more sinners or Irishmen will not try to overrun the area. In less than three hours, we had caught and kept our limit plus caught and released at least another four fish each. I don't even like fishing, yet if this is heaven, I am ready.

Neil cleaned the fish on the dock while a pair of seals, who perform for extra fish parts, provided the entertainment. Which is where the phrase was coined, "You want me to do what for a fin?" (My editor didn't get the joke because she is too young to know that a fin is old slang for five dollars. If you are too young . . . I apologize.)

Meanwhile, an angel named Maggie hovered about the kitchen of Salty Towers preparing another heavenly meal. Time flew by as it was filled with fresh seafood, incredible fresh lox and smoked salmon, plus excursions to Mom's Café and other exciting locations hidden about the community.

Neil later took us to Goldstream, where chum salmon come to spawn and die. Only in heaven is a creature allowed to die after spawning and before they have to look after the offspring, a fact that only the parents of teenagers would appreciate, but that is another story.

In heaven, these beautiful large fish turn gold and then die by the thousands, lining the riverbanks where the eagles, bears, and tourists who do not get a chance to fish with Neil drool over them.

Watching the beauty of the sunset on the ocean was truly heaven, and I was sad to realize my short visit there was over. I am comforted to know that when the kids take me down to the ice floes for that final journey, I will be drifting to somewhere as lovely as Sooke.

25 · The Legend of Stuart Caton

Does your family have reunions? You know, a gathering of relatives who normally avoid one another and only come so they aren't the subject of conversation?

In my family, each year seems to be a contest of who is most successful (at any number of things) and why grandma liked *me* best. One family started with who could produce the most kids, then it was who had the brightest kids, followed by whose kid would be paroled first. Is your family that competitive?

The Caton family, my mother's relatives, began reunions in the fifties when the family of ten would get together once a year to create stress in my grandparents' lives. Since then, we have gone through a number of competitions, the first one of which was who could have the most kids.

When one aunt and uncle started a string of twins, everyone else moved on to who had the cutest kid, but after four attempts, Mom dropped out of that one as well. On second thought, strike that sentence since my three sisters may read this column and disagree.

The contests continued up to who could arrive in the largest RV. When one of my sisters, who will remain anonymous, arrived with her husband, Rueben, in a motorhome slightly larger than B.C. Place Stadium, we all dropped out.

That brings us to last year's reunion at the Scott place, which can be found just outside the town of Lumby, B.C. I drove into town first to gas up, and the guy at the station wanted to know why I was there. (They still question newcomers in Lumby before they give you gas.)

As I left, he promised that if he noticed any strange people arriving in town, he would be sure to tell them they had missed the turnoff. I'm not sure what he meant by "strange." Perhaps it was a reflection on me or my sister, Darline, who seems to be well known in those parts.

Over fifty people showed up, and the competitions began. It started with the oldest group sitting in the shade and trying to remember the names of people they didn't like and hadn't seen for forty years.

Meanwhile, the youngest played tag amidst flying horseshoes. The kids went unseen by those throwing horseshoes, since they are old enough to need glasses but imagine they are too young to wear them.

The real competition started on the second evening, when traditionally an auction is held to raise funds for the food. I suggested I could write a column about the person who spent the most money, and soon the bags were flying around the room. Each bag had a name on it, and the bag that raised the most money would be the winner.

It was clear there were only three front-runners, the Caton cousins Gary, Bill, and Stuart. I was hoping Gary would win, because he's funny and it would be easy to write something outrageous about him, but somehow he placed out of the race. I think it was due to Bill, who dipped deep enough into his pocket to ensure that Stuart's bag total would be the largest, as he did not see winning himself as an honour.

Too bad Bill didn't win (or is it lose?); he's a Red Deer businessman who would also have been an easy target. Stuart, a well-respected central Alberta cattle farmer, tried to buy his way out as well by applying for a farm subsidy, but when it did not arrive in time, he sold a couple of cows to fund someone else's bag.

However, with the price of beef being what it is, the competition ended with the most money being raised in Stuart's name. I now had the task of finding something funny to say about this quiet and reserved man without offending him or all the other farmers who may read this column.

Farmers traditionally have a great sense of humour but may be getting a little testy these days between farm prices, the floods, and mad cow disease. In fact, I'm told that on the prairies, if parents leave the farm to their children, it is now considered a case of child abuse.

The condition of passing the farm along is not easily cured; for example, Stuart's son told me he wanted to stay at home and farm with his father, just as his grandfather Claude and his great-grandfather Glen Caton had done since 1903, before Alberta became a province. I am trying to imagine my kids, their kids, and their kids' kids saying, "I want to write a humour column for *North of 50*, just like my father before me."

Somehow being a farmer is more attractive, addictive, and demands an even greater sense of humour, so I now had to rise to the challenge of finding something funny to say about Stuart.

The weekend ended with cousins being scattered to the four winds, and the town of Lumby was safe once again. The competitions were over until the next time, when we all descend on some other unsuspecting town.

26 · The RV Reunion

We do not have family reunions as much as we have excuses to spoil the two long weekends of summer.

As I mentioned earlier, these reunions have become very competitive over the years.

The competition at the last one was "Who Has the Biggest Recreational Vehicle?"

When I arrived, I went straight to the washroom and discovered my brother-in-law and a cousin already engaged in a bragging competition. But I didn't know they were comparing motorhomes and, well, I got confused . . .

"So, whose is bigger?" my cousin, Trent, was asking. "Do you think yours is bigger than mine?"

My brother-in-law, Reuben, stared at him for a moment and answered, "Oh, yeah, mine is about twelve inches longer than yours is!"

I was stunned. Just then, Rueben turned to me, continuing, "How about yours, Layton?"

I guessed at what they were comparing and thought I should avoid this competition, so I said, "Mine's not that big . . . what about Les's? Do you think yours is longer than his?"

Rueben looked thoughtful. "Well, we never compared them side by side . . . but I think I've got him beat, too."

Trent jumped back in. "But Les's has a lot of power, his is a pusher, you know." A pusher?

Just then my nephew, Bob, came around the corner. Trent turned and said, "Bob, you still packin' your old big foot?"

Bob smiled and said, "No. I moved from a nine to a twelve. The wife said she was happy with nine, but I always wanted a bigger one."

"Did you say you went from nine to twelve?" I muttered. "Did it hurt?"

"Sort of," he said. "Last fall I ran it right into the back end of some lady from Vancouver and bent it."

That was a scene I didn't wish to envision.

"Bent it? I've heard Vancouver women are tough, but bent it?" I was still muttering.

"Yeah," he said. "I was in a hurry and not paying close enough attention. The next thing you know . . ."

"Wait! I don't want to hear any more." I was thinking this would be a good time to get out of the bathroom.

Then Rueben cut back in. "Hey, Layton, tell us about yours."

"Mine's nothing special," I said, still reluctant to join this competition.

"Well, is it a slider?" he persisted.

"Ah, yeah," I answered. "I guess you could call it a slider, but I prefer to think of it as a pusher."

"So how many does it accommodate at one time?" he asked.

I felt this was too personal, and besides, he knows I'm married and it only accommodates one. I was thinking of telling him where to park it, but he'd have to bend it.

So as I left the washroom, I said, "Hey, this has been interesting, but the wife needs help with the tent, and I have to put up the pole."

27 · Boomers

I used to be nervous about speaking in public. One of my first engagements was for a seniors' group after-dinner talk. I arrived so early that they put me in an adjoining room while the audience finished their meal. I took the opportunity to reread what I had planned to say, and of course, could not resist making changes.

Soon I was busy erasing and rewriting the entire talk. There was a big bowl of peanuts on the table, and I like to snack while I write, so there I was, focused on my work, writing with one hand and scooping peanuts up with the other.

I was lost in my thoughts when I realized that my hand was feeling around an empty bowl. I had eaten all the peanuts. I looked around, somewhat embarrassed, to see if anyone had noticed, and sure enough, there was a little old man sitting and watching me intently.

"I'm sorry. I seem to have eaten all the peanuts," I said apologetically.

"That's all right, sonny," he said. "Most of the people around here don't have their own teeth and can't eat the peanuts anyway. So they just suck the chocolate off and put them in that bowl."

Oh.

I was lying in bed the morning I turned fifty-five when my wife reached over and touched my hand. "Don't touch me. I'm dead," I grumbled.

"You're not dead. Why would you say you're dead?" she asked. I turned to her and explained, "Because nothing hurts."

So now I am like everyone else seeking the secrets to eternal youth. I was recently introduced to a product that increases the body's production of HGH, human growth hormone. The fellow promoting it said our body regenerates all our cells about once every three weeks, and by increasing the level of human growth hormone, we reverse the aging process. He said that age spots start to disappear, scars get lighter, and our body begins to heal and repair itself.

I told him that was decidedly not for me. I cannot imagine seeing my doctor every three weeks so he can keep renewing my vasectomy.

The salesman reassured me, however. He said it did not repair vasectomies, but I was skeptical. If it heals and removes scars, why not vasectomies? How does it know a good scar from a bad one? How does it know the difference between a cut on my hand and one on my privates?

It seems to me that since I went over the hill, I have begun to pick up speed. The good news is that smiles are aerobics for emotional health and grins are instant facelifts, so I am thinking that if you smile at my material, you will look younger and be healthier, and if you giggle or laugh hard enough it will give you enough exercise to replace a breast enhancement, and I should be compensated monetarily. So please, for all our sakes, laugh out loud.

Getting older is supposed to make you smarter and more mature, but I think that aging is too high a price to pay for maturity. Therefore, I am searching for a way to recapture my youth even if it means remaining immature. In the meantime, my research has uncovered new laws for getting older:

For the women, I discovered:
1. Some days are a waste of makeup, and all the hair spray in the world will not help.
2. There is always one more idiot than you expect and it will end up being the one you least suspect.
3. Everyone has a photographic memory, but some people do not have any film.
4. Most men seem normal until you get to know them.
5. If he says that you are too good for him, believe him.

For men, I've learned the following:
1. We should never give ourselves a haircut after three drinks.
2. If we must choose between two evils, we should pick the one we have never tried before.
3. The five essential words for a healthy, vital relationship "I apologize" and "you are right."
4. As soon as all the other parts feel good, our conscience begins to hurt.
5. Never pass up an opportunity to pee.

I also discovered that if you eat right and work out regularly, you will die anyway, so I instead simply try to weigh less than our refrigerator.

Now another group of seniors wants me to speak to them, and I must write my speech, so please pass me the peanuts quickly before they suck all the chocolate off.

28 · Your Mate as a Vehicle

If you had to pick a vehicle as your mate, which one would you choose? At a social gathering the other night, someone asked the question, and it raised a number of interesting ideas.

One woman said that she would like to spend her life with an Italian sports car, sleek and fast, hugging her curves tightly. Perhaps too tightly, I suggested. How will you keep it satisfied running up and down the same old road? What happens when it begins to look for a more challenging road or feels there are getting to be too many frost heaves and starts to look for a smoother surface?

No, I reflected, I do not think most women would remain happily married to an Italian sports car, to which an Italian woman added that she thinks they are overrated. She said they only perform well if you keep them revved high and are quick on the stick shift, which is fun at first but too much work over the long haul.

A second woman suggested she would want a new Chrysler wagon. You know, the one in the ads that carries a surfboard, a couple of two-by-fours, and a guitar amp, yet still outperforms that Italian sports car. She said the thought of having the big power plant throbbing as it idles in her driveway excites her.

It should be a red one too, she said, because red is exciting. And it must have leather seats, those ones that smell like Old Spice aftershave. I wonder if she will still be happy when the shine fades and it becomes hard to keep tuned, not performing as well as it did but still consuming more fuel than anything else in the neighbourhood. This is difficult. Think about it. Which would you choose?

Her husband felt that a mid-sized four-by-four pick-up is the right answer. The large bulky ones can be too hard to handle. He said you can dress them up yet throw them into four-wheel drive. They do get down and dirty, and no matter how deep the ruts, they just want to keep going.

They are also handy to have around the house because they can pack a ton of stuff, don't consume a lot of fuel, and the soft, comfortable interior is fun to snuggle into.

A third woman suggested that she would choose a motorcycle. Not just any motorcycle but the biggest and hardest to ride, a Harley Davidson. She wanted to feel the wind caress her hair, the vibration tingle her fingers and toes. She wanted to feel the surge of the big power plant between her legs come to life with a twist of her wrist.

Her husband asked if she would settle for a little Honda 50. She smiled, and they strolled off together, hand in hand.

I asked another friend what he would choose, and he mentioned a '56 T-Bird. But on second thought, he added, they were getting a little old, and in a perfect world, perhaps he should have something with lines that are more modern.

The new birds don't quite do it, but maybe a Mercedes sports coupe, the one with the nice-looking headlights. Great lines, soft leather seats that wrap right around you and become warm in chilly weather. He liked that idea but thought it might be a little high maintenance, as they require the best and most expensive parts and fuel.

Then he became concerned and asked, what if he couldn't keep it in the style to which it is accustomed? As it aged, would he be spending a fortune trying to keep it looking good? Would other guys always want to drive it? Maybe a guy should be happy with something a little plainer, he decided.

I said I thought my wife would choose a Hummer. That would be me, and I am not speaking about the wimpy, shiny GM makes; I'm talking about the drab green military ones. The biggest, squarest vehicle on the road. Like me, it consumes a lot, but it goes anywhere. It doesn't pretend to be sleek or fancy, yet stands out in a crowd.

It is simple and easy to love, even though most women feel it is completely impractical. Best of all, it doesn't wear out and will perform for years; at least that is what I choose to believe.

When my wife heard those comments, she laughed and suggested that she might be compelled to choose a Smart Car. She does not care that they are small, and she likes the idea they are built for one. They are not the fastest and do not have a very big power plant, but they are very efficient, can turn on a dime, and they are kinda cute in a funny sort of way.

Me, a Smart Car? I don't think so. Do you think there is a message there somewhere for me? The thought of it makes my hair hurt. I am beginning to think this was one of the dumbest questions I have ever been asked.

29 · The Dancer and the Border Cops

I somehow knew she was an exotic dancer even before she admitted it. Not that I would normally know what one looked like, but I had seen a glimpse of one on a CSI show and she just looked the type. It wasn't just her waist-long, bleached-blond hair, her small waist, her tall, slim look, or even her oversized bosom.

I think she was hauled into Homeland Security because of the way she was dressed. She was obviously not hiding anything. In fact, her state of dress looked as if she had been interrupted mid-show.

When she forced a smile as I sat down in the same area, I couldn't help but wonder who decided that plumping up the lips into a permanent pout was sexy. It occurred to me that should this young lady meet an early demise, they could recycle more of her than there would be left to bury.

She turned and continued talking to a young Asian lady seated beside her. I listened. The Asian woman held dual citizenship from Hong Kong and Canada, and apparently Homeland Security was concerned that if they let her into the States, they had no guarantee she would leave. I could see the risk to U.S. security, let one person from Hong Kong in and the next thing she would be mass-producing cheap radios, throwing hundreds of Americans out of work.

Both women had been in the holding pen for three hours while several uniformed, gun-toting officers scurried back and forth and the main man at the desk looked up occasionally to bark orders, such as letting me know I should not answer my cell phone.

I continued to wait patiently even after my flight had given the last boarding call. They called my name a couple of times, then exercised the agreement I have with the airline: if I do not show up on time, they are free to leave without me.

The man at the desk, the only thing between me and the United States, called me up again, and I thought I would finally receive the temporary visa I was seeking in order to legally collect for my speaking services while in the U.S. Unfortunately, that was not the case. Rather, he grilled me like a fresh fish.

First, he wanted to know what qualified me to speak for a fee. Then he grunted, fingerprinted me, and told me to sit down again.

The young ladies were still engaged in conversation when the man at the desk called the dancer to come up and bring her bags with her. He asked her several times if she planned to dance while in the States, which she repeatedly denied. Then, with the entire waiting area as an audience, he opened her bag and began to search it.

The officer announced to his colleague that he had discovered the dancer was packing her tools of the trade. He held up her underwear. My gawd, I thought, I'm packing underwear, too. I hope they don't conclude that I'm Joe Boxer, male dancer extraordinaire.

What if I showed up with no underwear, would they assume I'm the Great Streaker? Makes a person wonder what you ought to pack when travelling through Customs.

Meanwhile, the dancer's big lips began to tremble, and large, artificial tears began to flow. One tear must have finally touched the man defending America because he put her underwear down, took a quick look through the rest of her bag, and concluding she was not a major threat to his country after all, he let her proceed.

After telling the Asian woman that she had to leave within thirty days, the man at the desk finally let her in. At last, it was just him and me. He stared at his computer for several more minutes and then called me to come forward with my bags. He looked me over like it was the first time he had seen me, gave me my TN visa, and told me to proceed.

That's it? All that waiting for nothing, no questioning, no strip search, nothing? I was so happy I felt like dancing but restrained myself as I did not want him having second thoughts and questioning my underwear. So I just quietly stepped into U.S. territory.

30 · Armed and Dangerous

I would like to dedicate this column to my son Carson and all his associates. I am talking about the young men and women who stand in harm's way so that we might enjoy a better life. To the people who perform the most dangerous and difficult jobs in the country, I salute you.

The armed forces personnel, police, and firefighters have received a lot of recognition lately for the fine work they do, but we overlook the one group that works with the most violent offenders and without whom this country could not function.

People who police the streets are constantly in harm's way, but they have bulletproof vests, guns, Tasers, and other high-tech equipment. The young people I am talking about venture to work at a most ungodly hour of the day amidst weapon-wielding combatants, armed only with a whistle to referee youth hockey games.

While the public has a lot of respect and offers support to other policing agencies, they verbally abuse these teenage referees. Young men and women who don't worry about a salary cap, but work for little more than a Tim Horton's ice cap.

They put on the uniform that everyone loves to hate, yet without them there would be no national game. And their dream is to make it to the big leagues, where they throw themselves between the likes of Todd Bertuzzi and whomever he woke up disliking that morning. Or they put their helmets in front of stick-swinging Marty McSorley, who likens white helmets to golf balls.

A career where, if they turn pro, they can earn almost one-eighth of the salary paid to the lowest-priced player in the league. The good news is they can have their teeth replaced at the league's expense.

So the next time you see a twelve-year-old kid who stands six-foot-seven, weighs two hundred and forty-five pounds, and whose knuckles drag on the ground, instead of saying, "Wow, I wonder which team he plays for," think of the young man or woman with the whistle who will have to explain to him that using his stick to club another player from behind is a serious offence, and he must miss two minutes of the game.

Unless of course, he injures the other player, in which case he could be assessed a five-minute penalty. He could even be forced to sit out a game or two, if the injuries are life-threatening.

The young referee must explain this while maintaining his or her professional manner while half of the fans scream for the offender to be lynched and the other half scream that the ref is blind and the blow was justified because the victim had refused to share the puck.

So why do they do it? It is certainly not for the eight dollars per hour, but because of the character it builds and the other skills they learn. For example, only at a hockey rink can you learn to say complete paragraphs using only single-syllable words—and of course, have an opportunity to master hockey's favourite word.

Without the brave young people venturing out onto the ice amidst the armoured and armed warriors, protected only by their small plastic whistle, Canadians would have to spend Saturday nights watching basketball.

Meet the Family—Part Six

Shauna, my second oldest, has always been the worrier. When she was about six years old, she invited a friend for a sleepover.

Her friend's mother called to say that her daughter had never slept at anyone else's home because she had a bed-wetting problem, but that her little girl really wanted to stay with Shauna.

Shauna saw us put a plastic sheet under the cotton sheet on the top bunk and wanted to know what we were doing. After some discussion, we decided we should explain it to her. We took a great deal of care, stressing the importance of saying nothing if something should happen.

In the middle of the night, Shauna crawled into our bed, and when Myrna asked her why, she said, "I didn't want to say anything, but I keep thinking I hear her peeing. I **am** on the bottom bunk, you know."

That could be enough to keep even those of us who do not worry awake.

Today Shauna and Brian now have Kierra and Easton, their own two children—Who Shauna never puts to sleep in bunkbeds!

31 · What Is Your Sexual Number?

"What is your number?" is the actual question I was asked. I didn't know it had anything to do with sex at the time, so I added *sex* to the title in order to catch the attention of those of you who would have otherwise skipped over this piece. And it is an important piece, so read on.

I had to confess my naïveté and asked what she meant by "my number."

"I thought everyone knew what that meant," she added, making me feel even more out of touch. "It means how many partners you have had intimate encounters with?"

I explained that I am happily married and have been faithful to the same woman for the past twenty years, but she said, "No, I mean the total number for your life."

"I don't know."

"Of course you do. Everyone knows their number," she persisted.

At my age, it is becoming increasingly difficult to remember even having a life before I was married. I was at a loss for words. Besides, what business was it of hers and how do you answer a question like that anyway?

If you believe the movies today, a single man should have dozens; if I admit to fewer, will that make me seem like less of a man? On the other hand, if I admit to too many, what messages would that send? I resorted to my first instinct, asking her outright, "Why do you want to know?"

She said she was doing a survey and was finding that the average number for most mature adults (that means "north of fifty") is forty.

"So what is your number?" I asked.

"Nine. I have been stuck at nine for some time," she admitted, and I thought perhaps her problem was that she speaks with a German accent, most of her friends are German, and when they ask for her number, maybe they think she is rejecting them. (The German word for "no" is "nein." It's bad when you have to spell it out.)

In the small town where I came from, nine was a high number. We had names for a woman with a number that high. Not that we thought she was immoral, but our school was so small that if the number was over ten, it meant cousins or other family members were involved.

Nine. That could result in a number of problems. With this as a study topic, I am sure she could qualify for a number of federal research grants. But what if her research led her to a guest appearance on the David Letterman show and he asked her to list her top ten? She would have to list them all, even the bad ones, and she would still come up one short. How embarrassing would that be? You cannot lie on *The Late Show*: someone would know.

I could see she had a problem, but not one I could help her with, unless some of you men want to send in your résumés to help push her through this slump. There I go again, showing my naïveté. I should have said, "some of you readers."

"Do you feel your number is too low?" I asked.

"Not really, but I'm single. My best friend, who is my age and married, tells me her number is over forty. That's why I am doing this survey. Maybe my number is too low. What are your friends' numbers?"

I know my friends' golf numbers, both what they shoot and what they say they shoot. I know their phone numbers, their fax numbers, their cell numbers, and some of their house numbers. I know the number of wives they have had, the number of kids they have, and some of them have even shared the number of times they pee in a day, but that's for an entirely different column on what new and exciting things we have to talk about as we approach our golden years.

Quickly searching my memory bank, I could not remember a single conversation in which my friends and I sat around and discussed "*our number.*"

How can I continue to offer help and coaching if people keep coming up with problems I have never heard of? My research did not turn up one support group for people with too low a number.

People searching for lost kids have scooped up the milk carton idea, but maybe there is another food container on which these people could run their photos and plead for help. Bread doesn't have the right connotations and ketchup just doesn't seem right, either, but perhaps Alpha-Bits or Alphagetti would give up some space on their containers.

They could change the letters inside to numbers, now that has possibilities. They could run a photo with small text asking for someone out there to help these poor people get their numbers up.

32 · The Light Plan

My two front temporary crowns were giving me a little discomfort, and I was concerned they might be becoming infected. I was working at our lighting store in northern Alberta, where I do not have a doctor, so I trotted off to a walk-in clinic. I discovered the reason they are not called "walk-out" clinics is that it takes so long to actually see a doctor that you can no longer walk at all.

"It will be three to four hours before the doctor can see you." The young woman was the only smiling and friendly face in an office of over fifty people. Therefore, I decided to break out the computer and write this column while I waited.

Looking at all the people lined up, I began to think, if only I could line up customers and have them wait hours to give me their business, I would be a happy man. I wonder if doctors would be this busy if the clients had to pay directly for their services. Imagine how the government could help fuel the economy if it offered the same model to other industries.

Then it hit me: the three most important elements to support life are water, light, and air. Being in the lighting business, I am providing one of the three key elements. Therefore, the government should develop a light program that provides free lights to people when they need them.

Think about it, you wake up one morning feeling a little down or you are just sick of looking up at those same old lights. Under this new program, you would just drop by the store, pick up a couple of new fixtures, and presto, you would feel better again. I would certainly feel better, and the government would be happy because it costs less money than seeing a doctor. I can scarcely believe that someone has not proposed this before.

Of course, you should not rush into a new program like this without first thinking through all the different scenarios and the various problems that it may create. Otherwise, before you know it, someone will be lobbying for a two-tier light program.

Thinking like a doctor, I am tempted to support a system that will allow me to make more money from my richer clients rather than give everyone the same lights. On the other hand, I understand those with a social conscience and the argument that even the homeless should be entitled to the same lights as the rich. Is it fair to let some folks have higher quality lights just because they can afford to pay for theirs?

How would we keep track of unethical companies that might offer generic lights? Should we not be protected from cheap knock-offs that some big-box stores might bring in from third-world countries, and how would we keep alternative lighting stores from popping up everywhere?

We might also run the risk of experiencing the same problem the drug companies in the U.S. are experiencing, only in reverse. I am talking about big lighting stores that could locate in the U.S., and then offer cheap lights over the Internet, shipping them indiscriminately into Canada. We would have to set up a government agency or two in order to ensure the lights coming into our country not only emit the proper amount of light but also make people feel good about buying them.

The doctor's receptionist said I would be next, but before closing my laptop, I stopped to proofread what I had spent the last several minutes writing. I hope you have not already reached the same conclusion I did: I thought the infection was beginning to spread to my brain.

How could I have been so selfish as to think the government should just fund the lighting stores? They don't just fund doctors; they also fund a host of other medical specialists including some pharmacists and physiotherapists. We will have to increase the fees, of course, but it will be worth it because the program will now include interior designers who prescribe which lights to buy, electricians who install them, and someone from the disposal industry to not only remove the old fixtures but to counsel you on your loss.

As you can see, designing a comprehensive and universal lighting program is not as easy as it sounds, but I believe I have laid the groundwork. I just hope someone out there can take the idea, flesh it out, and get it through the right government channels.

Until then, if you are having lighting issues, stop by the store and, if I'm not still waiting at the doctor's office, I would be happy to prescribe something that will lighten up your day.

33 · And That, Your Honour, Is When I Decided to Murder Him

"And that, your honour, is when I decided to murder him . . ."

"Why did you say that?" My son Carson looked at me strangely.

"Oh, I'm just practising what I will say to the judge if you keep this up." He should have frozen with terror, but instead he just smiled and gave me the same look you might give a toothless old dog before patting his head and moving on.

Perhaps I should consider buying a chainsaw and goalie mask and placing them right beside my chair. A parent has to be creative in order to stay ahead of the kids. If they think you might be just a little crazy, you have a chance of keeping them off-guard.

In truth, Carson, who is approaching sixteen, is not a bad kid; he is just trying out his new James Dean, rebel without a clue, teenaged, the "world revolves around me" attitude. I am blessed with great kids, but although I used to have five theories on how to raise perfect children, I now have five children and no theories, but I digress.

Carson has actually become my hero, but don't tell him that. He plays sports the way I remember playing myself. (Of course, none of my family or friends remember me playing them that well.) As I watch him run into the end zone at least once a game, I struggle to relive the one time I ran in, or did I just make that up?

It seems the older I get, the better I was, and the more I tell my kids about the way I used to do it, the harder it is for me to remember the truth.

When Carson was seven, I'm convinced he said to himself, "I wonder how much money Dad has. I think I'll find out by taking up the most expensive sport", and he became a goalie.

My wife instituted a shared pay-as-you-go program to keep us out of the poorhouse. As a result, Carson had to get a job to help buy a trapper, a glove that costs more than most trappers can make in a season. That glove is for just one hand and a small part of the goalie's special "I-have-to-have" equipment.

True to his commitment of becoming a professional athlete by not working for money, he found he could earn money refereeing. The hardest part for him is determining in what sport to have a career: hockey, football, rugby, soccer, or just talking about it like Don Cherry. In fact, Carson would make a great Don Cherry: he knows more facts and trivia that anyone I know, and he never lets any of the facts get in the way of his opinion.

Carson is still only six-foot-one, so I told him that because I am taller, I am stronger. Then, just the other day, he beat me at arm wrestling. I had to feign injury to cover the loss.

I felt compelled to remind him that I gave him life and I can take it away. Then I looked over toward my chair, mentioning I would be getting a chainsaw soon. He smiled again and asked if I would need a hand starting it.

If Carson is my hero, Liam, our thirteen-year-old, is my idol. When the two boys stand side by side, with their shoulder-length hair and tall, lean bodies, they look like a throwback to a sixties British rock group.

At a recent family gathering, a cousin asked why I allowed them to have such long hair. "I finally I got the hair I wanted," I replied, "even if it is on my boys and not my ever-increasing bald spot." With so many other battles to fight, why pick the same one I fought with my dad?

The only disagreement we have is that I believe they should wash and comb it, at least once every lunar cycle. For some reason, it looks the wildest during the full moon.

Carson did not quite break us, so Liam took up the challenge by asking for music lessons. He thought, "What is the loudest, most expensive instrument to buy and most costly to transport around?" He settled on a drum kit. He is getting better at drumming although he still prefers to practise in the dark, when the moon is high.

Liam has not decided on a career. He thinks he would like to study bugs and insects or play in a band that looks like bugs and insects.

Liam promised me last year that even though he was turning thirteen, he would not become a teenager. He lied! I now have to revise my line and begin practising all over, "And that, your honour, is when I decided to murder *them*."

34 · Rules of the Range

The problem with being a stay-at-home dad is there is no manual outlining all the new responsibilities. Not that I read manuals much, nor would I admit to doing so; after all, I am a man, and reading the instruction manuals violates the male code. However, the stay-at-home dad manual would be good to have around for when nothing else seems to work.

One of the most challenging new homemaking chores for me was cooking. I thought I could cook, since I'd done my share when I was single and I did not mind filling in the odd time when the wife was not able make a meal.

However, that was part-time, like an amateur; now that I was spending a lot of time at home, it was time to turn pro and become a full-time master of the range. I had struggled to learn the rules of shopping for food, but I thought I could graduate to mastering the rules of how to prepare it easily.

I discovered quickly that there are three key areas to be conquered. First is what source of heat to use to cook the meal: barbeque, microwave, toaster oven, convection oven, easy-clean oven, self-clean oven, or range top.

I understood the barbeque and I knew how to warm leftovers in the microwave. The stovetop, I thought was just an indoor campfire, so it should be no problem either, but the oven? This was going to be a new challenge. As I stood looking at it, I realized that our oven has more controls than my Piper airplane, and I only had a pilot's license.

It was time to choose my fire. I was ready for the challenge but daunted by the fact that women have evolution on their sides. Women have developed their fire skills over hundreds of generations, but men went directly from fire pit to barbeque.

Oh, there was a short stint with the stovetop when I was single, but the only thing I used was a frying pan. I cooked bacon and eggs for breakfast, a fried cheese sandwich for lunch, steak and potatoes for supper, and when eating alone, I did not have to use dishes.

I could eat directly out of the frying pan, give it a wipe, and leave it on the stove for the next meal. That left the oven free to use as a spare storage compartment, and it was especially good for warming up underwear during a cold prairie winter.

A woman will put up with meals like the ones I cooked when they are single, but once a man utters those two little words, "I do," those days are done.

Once married, a man learns quickly that eggs have too much cholesterol and cheese too much fat, as does anything fried. The steak is not good for you, because not only is it grilled, it is red meat. I began to realize why the cows go mad.

If I were going to be a modern, healthy cook, I would have to learn the five basic rules of the range:

Rule 1: Not everything you put on the stove can come out of a can, and eggshells count as cans.

I am not sure who invented that rule. At least one ingredient has to be fresh. That became a problem, as I could not find fresh creamed corn. The second problem is that I tend to put fresh stuff in the bottom drawer of the fridge, where I promptly forget about it. Although it tends to get greener and fuzzier, it no longer counts as fresh.

Rule 2: You can put brown sugar in everything.

I am on a one-man crusade to prove it. I've found that brown sugar is the universal secret ingredient. You can add it to anything, and it only improves the taste. There are no downsides and no side effects. (And do not bring up the argument that the brown sugar may be why I am 275 pds—I'm just big-boned.)

Remember, men, it is important to wipe the cupboard thoroughly and carefully with a wet dishcloth after using brown sugar. Women can spot those little brown specks a mile away. My wife often looks like one of the characters on CSI as she looks through her magnifying glass digging out a speck of sugar from between the burners with her tweezers. "And what have we here?" she inquires over the top of her magnifier.

Rule 3: At least one item must be prepared from a recipe.

There are many problems with recipes. First, women think you should follow them. But that's like reading a manual, which should only be done when something does not turn out right. I find if I look quickly at a recipe, I can get the gist of it and then can wing it from there.

The key is to get the essence of what the recipe calls for, and then add ingredients you like such as molasses, onions, garlic, and more brown sugar.

Rule 4: To be a real cook, you have to use the oven at least once a week.

I found this to be very difficult at first. Once I discovered nachos, however, it was easy and delicious. If you simply spread grated cheese on taco chips, you will be reminded about the fat. But if you cut up a few peppers, spread on some onion, and add hamburger with molasses, it qualifies, and no one comments about the two kilograms of cheese.

Rule 5: A real master of the range should cook with at least three burners on at the same time.

I know you will find this is a problem if you do not have three frying pans, and you may ask, why would I cook my food separately if I have the large twenty-four-inch pan?

I do not have the answer to that, but I do know how to get around the difficulty. Put two small pots on the back burners with a little water and low heat. If you cover them with a lid, few people are rude enough to reach over a hot pan to see what you have cooking. That will free up your attention to concentrate on the big pan at the front.

Remember, not all men can master the range right away, and that's fine as long as you produce something the wife can brag to her friends about. Coming up with a tasty and attractive meal is not that difficult if you simply follow those five simple rules.

Meet the Family—Part Seven

"Is the story of Adam and Eve true?" Liam asked on the way home from his evening church group.

"I think it must be," Myrna said.

"But they didn't write things down then, so how do we know about it?" he continued.

"Well, they passed the stories down through the generations from one reliable source to another," Myrna replied.

"But Adam and Eve only had two boys, right?"

"Yes."

"And one boy killed the other, right?" Again Myrna replied yes, not quite sure where this was going.

"Well, then," our eight year-old continued, "wouldn't that make your reliable source a murderer?"

35 · Kelowna is Burning

I was attempting to write my monthly humour column but I was unable to find anything funny to say about the Okanagan Valley wildfires of the summer of 2003. I kept trying, but nothing would come.

The fire closest to us, the Okanagan Mountain Park Wildfire, had been raging for several days and was now threatening the outskirts of our city. Forest fires do not enter a city, do they?

The TV was on in the background when I suddenly heard the announcer say that our neighbourhood was now officially on alert. She went on to say that at any time the RCMP could issue an evacuation order, and we would have only one hour to respond.

Even if the fire did begin to encroach on the city, I thought it impossible that it would come this far, but still we reluctantly began packing both vehicles with our treasures. I suggested to the family that we assess everything and quickly categorize each item into two groups: (1) the treasures we could not replace, and (2) the things we might enjoy shopping for again.

As I thought about our family on a shopping spree to replace most of the things we now had, I suggested that if Sears knew about this plan, they would have been cheering for the flames.

Liam, our eleven-year-old, emerged from his bedroom packing a homemade lamp with a cedar base and a runway marker light mounted. "I know this is just a lamp and takes up a lot of room, but Grandpa made it for me. Can I take it?" he asked.

Of course we let him, that lamp is a real treasure. Several other inexpensive items with enormous sentimental value, as well as photo albums, filled the vehicles to the point that there was no room for the fur coat or nice furniture.

With the cars packed, we sat down to watch the ongoing news coverage, but the call did not come, so we prepared to turn in for the night. For the past several days, the summer sun had been little more than a large orange ball hanging behind a curtain of dense smoke. The smoke was so thick that it lined our nostrils, and everything stank.

The dogs, like most creatures that sense fire, refused to go outside for any longer than it took to dash to their favourite corner of the yard and take care of business. Back in the house, they followed Myrna from room to room as though they knew we might soon be evacuating and were afraid we might leave them behind.

The yard resembled a soft winter snowfall in August as the white ash covered everything, although the boys were quick to point out it was not as much fun to run through barefoot. At first, it was interesting to have a forest fire so close. We could safely view it from across the lake while I recounted to the boys the story of the forest fire I fought near Rocky Mountain House in 1969. It had become something of a legend over the years (if only in my own mind), so I couldn't be held responsible for any embellishments.

Back in Kelowna, the media reported that more and more people were losing their homes. An uneasy feeling settled over the city. Everywhere, people talked about the fire. Families were afraid to leave home in case the evacuation notice came and they were not there to grab their last few precious items. Evacuees moved or drove as though they were in a trance. They had hollow, blank looks on their faces as their bodies went through the motions while their minds were elsewhere. There was deep concern now that maybe just maybe—they could not stop the fire.

Now that we were officially on notice, we never ventured far from a TV or radio. As the evening wore on, we could see the flames clearly from our back deck. Gordon Drive, at the end of our street, was alive with fire trucks, emergency crews, and a steady stream of people leaving their homes and heading for the evacuation centre. The normally quiet street in front of our house was teeming with people; at one point a tailgate party started up as looky-loos came for a closer inspection.

Liam and Carson, our sons, stubbornly resisted going to bed. Instead, they stayed up until the wee hours listening to the news and watching through the back door as flames soared high into the night sky.

Friday morning we took the boys and went to work, but the office was filling up with furniture, suitcases, and boxes as colleagues brought in their personal belongings and pets for safekeeping. It was impossible to work, so we returned home to wait. The wind suddenly picked up and the news reported that the fire had jumped the fireguards and was running wild. Finally, the RCMP arrived in the neighbourhood with a loudspeaker, telling us we had to vacate immediately. The anxiety that accompanies anticipation vanished. It was replaced with a surge of energy from the stress of the situation.

We grabbed armloads of clothes and the computer hard drive and stuffed them into the last voids left between the boxes, and, like refugees, we prepared to join the long line of cars leaving the neighbourhood. One neighbour stopped, rolled down his window, and asked if we had any marshmallows they could toast from their back deck. His attempt at humour brought forced smiles as everyone tried to make light of what was happening. The tension in the air was even thicker than the smoke.

As we looked around one last time, someone commented that it was a shame we had to leave the bikes behind as we had bought them only a few weeks before. Carson asked if he and Liam could ride our bikes out, explaining that while their own mountain bikes could be easily replaced, the special new recumbent bikes that Myrna and I had bought were hard to find. Liam joined in, asking, "Can we ride them out for you?"

Although the traffic was heavy, it was moving slowly and we could see that they truly did want to help, so we agreed. We would wait for them at a strip mall on the other side of the evacuated area. They donned their helmets, put their backpacks on the rear carriers, and started down the street.

A couple of neighbours who were frantically packing their belongings into their cars stopped for a minute as someone shouted out, "Way to go, guys!" They were soon joined by other neighbours who applauded as the boys rode by. I was proud of our boys because their thoughtfulness and unselfishness gave our neighbours a few moments of pleasure amidst all the tension.

Leaving the bikes in a friend's garage on the other side of the city, we decided to spend the night in Vernon, a city forty-six kilometres north of us. Before leaving Kelowna, we stopped on a high hill overlooking the city and could hardly believe what we were seeing. The flames stretched over twenty kilometres from the lake in the southwest around to the east side of the city.

Although some distance away, the flames were clearly visible, leaping a hundred metres into the air and then even higher as they hit a home or some other flammable fuel. The entire night sky glowed red and orange like a beautiful sunset. Hundreds of other people stood in silence, watching awestruck at the forces of nature before quietly moving on.

After one night in Vernon, we found it too stressful to be away from our city and friends. Somehow we felt as if we should be sharing this time together with them, so we returned to Kelowna the following morning.

We didn't know how to occupy ourselves, and we certainly did not want to work. Smoke still choked the city and the media were now reporting that the fire had destroyed numerous homes. We joined other zombies cruising through big stores, not shopping, just moving aimlessly as though we had entered a twilight zone. When we did stop to talk to other displaced folks, it was always about the fire, repeating newscasts we had heard although it seemed no one was really listening.

Some tried to escape the situation by burying themselves in their work while others kept busy as volunteers. It was as though time truly stood still. And everywhere, the sounds of the newscasts filled the air as all TVs and radios were tuned to the local media, which reported non-stop.

Local merchants opened their businesses, offering extra services, often at no charge. McDonald's offered free coffee and a young man working at Tim Horton's gave us free cookies as he explained somewhat matter-of-factly that his family had lost their home the night before. It was surreal.

The experience reminded me of the first Gulf War when the TV remained tuned to the news all day until it became addictive, even though the same clips were playing over and over.

The video coverage was incredible but stressful, yet we continued to watch, looking for news of our home. We felt the fire itself would not come that far into the city, but feared the burning embers could set fire to roofs in neighbourhoods not directly threatened.

Back in 1969, the fire boss had ordered several of my friends and me to start a backfire, in order to destroy the long grass in the fields at the edge of our Alberta town. The strategy was that the forest fire racing toward us would run out of fuel and would be stopped. Unfortunately, he did not anticipate the changing winds and all crews spent the next forty-eight hours on the line, but we did prevent the fire from destroying Rocky Mountain House. Now some critics were insisting the Kelowna fire department should take the same action.

The professionally trained fire crews working hard to save Kelowna knew what they were doing; yet some armchair quarterbacks continued criticizing them. The public, the great silent majority, responded to the critics with signs that began appearing everywhere on light posts, roofs, school fences, front yards, and reader boards proclaiming our firefighters as heroes and thanking them for their efforts. Cars and trucks appeared with Canadian flags flying, and the drivers tooted when they passed police officers, firefighters, army personnel, or anyone else involved in the effort.

Overnight, fire chief Gerry Zimmerman become a local celebrity with his reassuring manner. He continually praised the men and women who were on the front lines.

The temperatures were in the high thirties Centigrade, and those near the fire experienced even more intense heat. Combined with the warmth of extra protective coveralls, it was almost unbearable.

The grit and ash continued to fall down the backs of the firefighters' necks and mix with their sweat, making conditions almost intolerable, yet they persevered. But though they continued working, their actions were thwarted. Many kept working in neighbourhoods they were assigned, despite knowing they were losing their own homes in other areas.

We were witnessing a community coming together. Not just the people of Kelowna, but other folks streamed in from communities across the country as personnel and crews. Those who could not help with the fire offered other services including a community rain dance in one of the downtown parks. Others opened their doors to strangers, offering to house them for the duration of the evacuation.

Finally a small rain fell, bringing down the temperature, but the front, still several kilometres long, advanced toward Gallagher's Canyon. We could see black smoke rise as the fire devoured fourteen of the eighteen gorgeous old wooden railway trestles that spanned Myra Canyon. The rail lines that had snaked back and forth a hundred years before had long ago disappeared, leaving only their historic trestles as part of the Trans-Canada Trail. Now, they, too, were lost forever.

We were at the registration centre set up at a local school, making plans to get a room for the night when news came that residents of our neighbourhood could return home, although we were to remain on alert status. It was late, and we were the only family to return home that night.

We felt alone in a silent and blacked-out community, and as we stood outside in the August heat, smoke floating through the streets, goose bumps forming. It felt as though a whole city of people had suddenly disappeared.

It felt good to be back in our home even though the smoke was now thicker than before, burning the nose and eyes. We kept the doors and windows closed tightly, and despite the fact we were still under the one-hour evacuation notice, we began putting our possessions away. We decided that we wanted to return to some sort of normalcy, and we were optimistic that we would not have to repeat the process.

The fire had been held back several blocks from our neighbourhood, but thousands of other people were still banished from their homes. In all, 250 families lost their homes, including several of our friends.

For days, we lived with the steady chop of helicopters flying over the house and dangling large water buckets below them, followed by large, low-flying water bombers reminding us we were still at war.

Kelowna came together and neighbours responded without panic. Strangers helped one another and, as one neighbour said, it was typically Kelowna, a casual evacuation in a laid-back style.

The fire is history now, the crews have gone home, and the loggers are harvesting the blackened sticks that were once the forest of Okanagan Mountain Park. The steady noise of concrete trucks and power saws has replaced the silence of chimneys that marked where houses stood, and hammers are beating strongly, like a heart telling the world Kelowna is alive and growing again.

Daily life has returned to normal, and I am beginning to think of funny things to write about again.

This article appeared in several publications across western Canada and is dedicated to the bravery of all the firefighters, police, and armed forces that came to our assistance and especially to the citizens of Kelowna, who remained calm and pulled together to maintain an orderly society in an extraordinary time.

36. Live, Love and Laugh

I wanted to write a column for my dad, Robert Park, when he passed away, but how can anyone write a humour column about the passing of a loved one? Then I remembered that Dad would have been disappointed if I wrote it any way other than light-hearted.

Dad use to tell us how he once came home on leave during WWII, his father, Pop, picked him up at the train station and let him drive home. When they came to a gate, both were too cold to get out and open it, and Pop said, "If I were driving someone else's car and came to a gate, I'd crash right through it." That was all Dad needed to encourage him, even though it meant spending the rest of his leave fixing a fence.

Even the last few weeks of his life, Dad continued to spread his humour and laughter. When the nurses would apologize for hurting him during treatment, he would apologize back for reacting, and then tease them with some smart comment.

For fifty-five years, laughter filled Mom and Dad's home. That laughter was a gift they passed along to all their children. It seems like yesterday we were all going to weddings, then attending children's birthday parties, graduations, and then more weddings. Now we are facing our own mortality as our friends and parents begin to pass away. Recently we have begun to question what is in store for us, and many of us are beginning to rediscover our spiritual roots.

Dad would have been one of those people who say they don't go into churches for fear of the roof caving in. But he never uttered the words because one time, while fighting a fire at our town's Christian Reform Church, he was squatting in front of a dormer window on the roof, holding the end of the hose alone when someone turned the water on and the pressure threw him into the burning church. The roof caved in moments after he stumbled out the front door.

He may not have been a regular at church, but Dad knew right from wrong. He taught his family honesty and integrity and lived by the golden rule. Although I, too, do not attend church as often as I should, and at times can be somewhat cynical, I would describe myself as spiritual or at least in search of my spirituality.

Again in his passing, Dad has given his family a gift of faith and hope. He was not on medication and was very lucid up until the last day, yet a couple of days earlier he had seemed to be in deep thought when he suddenly turned to Mom and said, "Where did Mother go?" He believed that his mother, who died over twenty years before, had been sitting with him.

On the last day, he again asked Mom about the presence of his brothers Howard and Arlan and his sister-in-law Phil (who had all passed away over the last couple of years) without asking about the surviving members of the family.

Finally, during that last day, he looked up past me, staring, raising his arms stiffly and holding his hands open like a child wanting to be picked up. My sister Lori asked, "What do you see, Dad?" When he didn't answer she asked again, "What do you see?"

He ignored her as though he was concentrating on something else, and finally lowered his arms and closed his eyes. He never spoke again. He passed in and out of consciousness for the rest of the day, and finally went to sleep forever. Immediately after he died, a strange sense of peace pervaded the room. He gave us the sense that we need not fear what we all have to eventually face.

On that last day, he also asked what kind of car Pop had. Although his father had passed away over thirty years before, it was as if he was trying to communicate with family that had predeceased him.

If it was Pop who had come to take him home, it was his wife and children who prayed that when he arrives at the Pearly Gates, they are open, because we know what Pop would say as they approached, and Dad would be up there still probably fixing the fence.

Starting on that day, we knew there would be a lot more laughter in heaven. And while no one relishes the thought of death, we look forward to the day we are all with him again. Thanks for seventy-eight years of laughter, Dad.

Dedicated to Robert James Park of Vernon, B.C., December 15, 1925–May 12, 2004

About the Author

Col. Layton Park C.Ht. CPBA, CPVA, RET

Layton Park spent years studying human behaviour in business and sales. He works with a number of large sales organizations, sports teams, and individual clients looking to make positive changes through application of affirmations, hypnosis, and visualization techniques as well as working a business consultant.

His work has taken him to all parts of the globe. In the former Soviet State of Kazakhstan, he acted as consultant to several companies seeking to change to a western style of business.

Layton began his own design-build company in 1975 and grew it into a business with more than 80 direct employees and several contractors. He also owned a successful real estate company and served as president of the local real estate board.

Layton has been a partner in several service-focused businesses. He is an active partner in Max-U. Inc. and GPS 4 Biz (providers of training and speaking programs), in Parkline Services (a development company), in LAMP Land Inc. (a lighting and décor business); and in The Canadian Hypnosis Institute. He also serves as silent partner in a manufacturing business.

Layton has spoken on business topics across Canada, the U.S., Mexico, and Kazakstan. He has authored a number of books and pens monthly humour columns for two Canadian periodicals. He is past president of the Canadian Authors' Association, Kelowna branch.

Layton's latest book, *Get Out of Your Way*, is available everywhere. This is a serious book on how to set and achieve goals, incorporating the author's years of experience as a successful business owner, speaker, and observer of human behaviour.

The honorary title of Colonel was conferred on Layton by Paul Patton, Governor of Kentucky.

Layton enjoys skiing and playing in the Okanagan with his family. An aviation enthusiast, he has flown his airplanes over 480,000 kilometres across the great Canadian north.

Layton is available for educational, inspirational, and humourous public presentations. If you'd like to have him address your group, contact him at <u>Info@max-u.com</u>.

Books by Layton Park

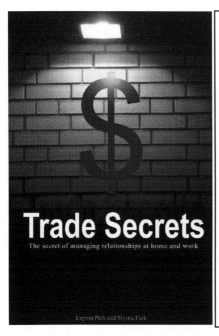

Trade Secrets
Layton Park and Myrna Park
The secret of managing relationships at home and work
This compelling business parable is about a tradesman who, together with his wife, builds a very successful business. That is until the day the three division managers tell him he has to make a choice between them and keeping his wife involved in the business.
Published by iUniverse
ISBN 978-0-9732111-2-2
6 x 9—120 page—2010

If You Are Going To Lead Don't Spit!
This book is a collection of motorcycle stories from Layton's humour columns in the Busted Knuckle Chronicles. The lessons in leadership in each story remind us that leaders are everywhere and instrumental in everything we do.

Published by iUniverse
ISBN 978-0-9732111-5-3
6 x 9—81 page—2010

Chicken Coop...
for a Rubber Sole

This book is collection of stories from Layton's columns in North of Fifty. These humorous stories are great short reads, ideal for airports or traveling where you may want to enjoy something light and fun. This book is an ideal inexpensive gift that can be easily re-gifted and enjoyed by people of all ages.

Published by iUniverse
ISBN 978-0-9732111-6-0

Don't Drink the Kool-Aid

How big business, government and religion use hypnotic techniques to influence their followers.

This book, scheduled for release Spring 2011 is a "must-read", for anyone wanting to position their organization in the minds of their customers and employees or wanting to understand how other big institutions are doing so to them.

Advance orders are available from the publisher in quantities of 20 for only $200 plus shipping.

Contact info@max-u.com

Get Out of Your Way
Unlocking the Power of
Your Mind to Get What You
Want
or—How to Remove
Limiting Beliefs Through the
Power of Self-Hypnosis
Trade Paperback
9780738710525
6 x 9-216 pages
Published March 2007 by
Llewellyn—New Worlds of
Body, Mind & Spirit